ONLY WHEN SHE SLEEPS

By:

Amanda Kilkenny

Printed in the United Kingdom
First Printing, November 2025

ISBN 978-1-0369-6447-4
Edited by: G.M. Parrillo
Cover Art by: Amanda Kilkenny
www.inkboundsociety.com
The Inkbound Publishing
Gort, Co. Galway, Ireland

Reviews are the key to an Independent Authors success. Please feel free to post your review on both Amazon and Goodreads. Thank you for your consideration.

Dedication

To my nightmares and the insomnia that haunted me, thank you for being both tormentor and research partner, for the endless late-night collaborations. But also, sincerely, fuck you.

To Gina, Roma, and mo anamchara, thank you for coaxing me back to the light when I nearly married the dark.

And to my Inkbound family, thank you for being the chorus in my chaos, the many voices that keep the realm alive.

Prologue

They say dreams are windows into the soul.

I used to believe that. Back then, it wasn't just a saying to me, it was a promise. Like if I leaned close enough, pressed my face right against the glass, I could see something vast and shimmering waiting on the other side.

When I was younger, when mom was still alive, she'd whisper it to me at bedtime like a secret. That dreams held the truth, memory and magic. That gods lived in that space between waking and sleep, and they whispered to those who listened. She told me once about a fisherman who sleep-walked into the sea at dawn and came back three days later with salt in his eyelashes and a voice full of riddles. Another night, it was a woman who could only speak in the language of birds after she dreamed of flying. Her stories bled into each other until they felt more real than daylight.

Back then, I clung to her words like lifelines. We lived in a house by the sea, battered by wind and the smell of salt. I remember wildflowers growing through cracks in the stone walls and mom humming old lullabies under her breath while brushing my hair. She was strange and beautiful and full of stories, the kind of woman people in our town gossiped about when they thought she couldn't hear.

She could. She just didn't care.

She used to tell me I was special. That I had a gift. That if I listened closely, the world would speak to me in symbols and signs. That I came from a long line of women who carried something ancient. I never understood what she meant. Not really. But I believed her. Because when mom looked at me, it was like she saw the whole universe reflected back. Once, I found a smooth grey stone shaped like a crescent moon on the shore. I ran to her with it, certain it was nothing, and she only smiled like I'd brought her proof of something she'd been waiting to see. Lightning flashed on the horizon long before the rain came, pale white ribbons snapping against the dark. Mom stood at the doorway, watching the water like she was counting each wave.

I was nine the night everything changed.

The storm came in quickly, thunder rolling in from the sea. It sounded like the sky was being torn open. The kind of storm that rattled the windows and made the air feel too thick, too charged. I remember the smell of it, salt and something sharp, metallic, like the air had been cut open and left bleeding.

Our house wasn't big, but it felt enormous that night. Too many shadows. Too many places for sound to echo. I was curled on the sitting room rug with a blanket over my shoulders, watching the lightning stutter against the walls while my mother paced the hallway, muttering words I couldn't understand. The rug was scratchy under my bare legs, the pattern twisting into strange shapes each time the lightning hit. I kept finding faces in them, all of them looking the wrong way.

She kept glancing at the mirror. The big one in the hallway. The one I wasn't allowed to touch. Once, when I was small, I'd pressed my palm to its surface and she'd yanked me back so hard I cried. She'd knelt in front of me, her voice tight, saying only, "Don't." No reason. No explanation.

Something about that storm scared her in a way I'd never seen before. I opened my mouth to ask what was wrong, but the question sat on my tongue like a stone. She wouldn't answer, and I wasn't sure I wanted to know. Not in the usual way, not thunder or flickering lights. No, she was afraid of something else. Something inside the house. Something that didn't belong anymore.

The wind howled like it had teeth, like it was trying to claw its way through the walls. The lights flickered once, twice, then died, leaving the house soaked in dark. Shadows stretched where they shouldn't have been, curling along the floorboards, slipping over the doorframes like they were waiting for permission to enter.

And I remember my mother's face. The way her voice dropped into a register I'd never heard before. The way she knelt, hands shaking, and whispered my name like it might be the last time.

"Róisín. Go. Hide. Don't come out until I say. No matter what you hear."

I did what she said. I curled myself into the cupboard under the stairs, hands clamped over my ears, heart thudding so loud I was sure it would give me away.

For a second, I thought I heard my name, faint, dragged like it was coming from somewhere impossibly far away. My palms pressed harder over my ears.

And then…***silence***.

Not just the absence of sound. Not the quiet of a storm fading. A heavy, suffocating stillness. The kind that presses in behind your eyes and fills your mouth like water. A silence that felt wrong.

And after that… ***nothing***.

No footsteps. No voice calling me back.

No dreams. Not ever again.

I have one blurred flash from between the cupboard and the morning after, the smell of hot iron, the scrape of something heavy dragging across the floor, a glimpse of blue fabric moving where it shouldn't. Then it's gone.

★ ★ · ★ · ★ · ★ · ★

I was sent to live with my dad and sister after that night. The car ride was quiet. I remember the rain streaking sideways across the windows, blurring the cliffs until they looked like they were melting into the sea. I kept glancing back, half-expecting to see someone standing there, watching us leave.

My dad. The man who was suddenly responsible for two daughters, one he barely remembered how to hold. He hadn't been around much before it happened, always somewhere else, always just out of reach. I used to wonder if maybe he was allergic to softness, to small talk. To the clumsy affection of children. To me. Like he could only stomach the shape of a family from a distance, so long as no one got too close.

He didn't talk about mom. He didn't want to. He didn't like when I did.

Every time I tried, whether it was a memory, a question, something small like the way she used to hum while brushing my hair, his face would change. Not violently. Just… tighten.

Like the sound of her name scraped against something raw inside him. His hands would clench, not to strike, but to steady himself. Like whatever he was holding back might spill out if he breathed too deep.

I learned quickly to stop asking.

He moved us to the city. A flat on the second floor that always smelled of damp and bleach and whatever cheap cleaning spray had been used to cover the rot in the walls. The radiators clicked but rarely produced heat. The windows never sealed properly. At night, the sound of traffic crawled up from the street and made itself at home in my bones.

My sister Fiadh had already been living with him. She knew the rhythms of that place. The shape of his silences. The weight of the spaces where conversation should have lived. There was something brittle but familiar between them, a quiet understanding built in my absence. And when I arrived, pale and empty and carrying whatever my mother had left behind in me, I didn't fit.

We shared a bedroom for a while. Two beds, pushed to opposite walls. Her side was always warm, posters taped unevenly to the walls, books stacked like they were mid-thought, clothes in soft, familiar piles. Mine stayed neat. Cold. Too quiet. We spoke, sometimes. Ate meals at the same table. Laughed when it didn't cost too much. But I always felt like I'd stepped into a story already halfway through, like I was a new line of dialogue in a script that didn't need rewriting.

They had a history I didn't belong to. One evening at dinner, Fiadh made a joke about something from years before, and they both laughed before glancing at me, like they'd forgotten I was there.

My father was a quiet man with tired eyes. Not a peaceful kind of quiet, not the kind that makes you feel safe. His silence was dense. If he ever believed in magic, or stories, or anything soft and golden, then he'd buried that belief deep, somewhere far out of reach.

Still, I could feel it - even then.

The absence.

Like standing in front of a door I wasn't allowed to open. Like something was missing and no one had the courage to name it. I told myself it was grief. That the aching space I carried was just the shape my mother left behind. But there was more to it. There always had been.

I learned how to be small. How to fold myself into corners. To make myself easy, quiet and unthreatening. If I could stay still enough, soft enough, maybe I wouldn't stir whatever it was he saw when he looked at me too long.

I shrank into myself. Let the silence fill the gaps. Pretended not to feel how the weight inside me shifted, growing louder each year.

I always thought it was because I looked like her.

The same unruly waves of dark hair. The same high cheekbones. The pale skin that never flushed, even in summer. But it was my eyes that made people stop. mom used to call them emeralds. The kind of green that didn't belong in this world.

They unsettled him the most.

Sometimes I'd catch him watching me. Once, I woke in the night and found him standing in the doorway, not moving, just looking. His face was unreadable, and he stepped back before I could speak. Like he could still see her flickering beneath the surface of my skin. Like the past hadn't left at all, just curled up inside me and waited.

I didn't understand it then.

Not the way he moved around me like I was something fragile. Not the way his silence always thickened when I laughed too loud or looked too much like her.

Even as a child, before I understood what had been taken from me, nights were the longest thing in the world. I used to count them in objects, not hours, the shadow of the wardrobe growing taller against the wall, the way the crack in the ceiling shifted shape if I stared at it long enough, the second-hand tick of the clock in the kitchen that travelled under the floorboards to find me.

I made rituals without meaning to. Walk the hallway twice before bed. Check the locks three times, even when Dad was already asleep. Keep the lamp on until my eyes burned from it, because darkness made the flat feel like it had more corners than walls.

On the worst nights, I would lie on my back and try to imagine what dreaming might feel like. Was it colour? Was it sound? Did it taste of salt like the air at mom's house by the sea, or of the chalky pills Dad kept in the bathroom cabinet? I would make pictures in my head and hold them there until they wavered, until I felt the edge of sleep, and then nothing. Always nothing.

Sometimes I'd think I saw shapes when I closed my eyes. Lines and curves like a map drawn in the dark, or the faint green afterimage of a light switched off. Once, the smell of chamomile drifted in from the kitchen, not the tea Dad drank, but the fresh kind mom used to crush between her fingers, warm and bitter. It was so sharp, so sudden, that my chest ached as if she had just been in the room. I opened my eyes to catch her. Of course, there was no one there.

These little hours before morning always stretched the thinnest. It felt like I could push my hand through the air and touch something that wasn't mine, that didn't belong to this life. But if I reached too far, it might notice me.

So, I stayed still. Always still.

Years passed. I learned how to read EEGs before I could drive. Watching those sharp, jagged lines record someone else's dreams was like looking at a language I would never speak, a heartbeat that didn't belong to me.

I got good at pretending everything was fine. Good at studying. Good at working. Good at becoming someone people didn't have to worry about. I built routines, controlled everything I could. I threw myself into science like it might save me. The sharp edges of logic and data and clean conclusions felt safer than stories. Numbers didn't ask questions, they didn't whisper. They didn't leave shadows where there shouldn't be any. Numbers let me pretend I was ordinary.

But the silence never went away.

Sleep became the thing I feared and envied the most. Because when I closed my eyes, there was nothing. No images. No symbols. No fragments of the strange stories my mother once whispered into my hair. Just void.

People call it dreamless sleep like it's peaceful.

It's not. It's a kind of exile.

Oh, how I envied people who dreamed. The way they laughed about it at work, trading strange images over coffee. Comparing symbols. Piecing together nonsense that still felt like something. A language I couldn't speak. A world I couldn't touch.

I even envied their nightmares. The way they woke shaken but alive. At least nightmares meant something was still reaching for them. Speaking to them. They weren't alone in the dark.

But me?

I had nothing.

Only black.

A cold, indifferent nothing that wrapped around me like I didn't belong in the same world as everyone else. Like I was locked out of something. Something that belonged to other people but not to me. Like I was exiled from my own soul.

Chapter One

Running on Empty

Roisin

I haven't slept in days.

Three, maybe four. Possibly five. I stopped counting somewhere between the second panic attack and the third microwaved dinner. My brain is a frayed wire sparking in the dark, hot in places, dead in others, and I keep waiting for it to short out completely.

Time is useless when your brain refuses to shut off. It folds, collapses, repeats. The hours bleed together like bad watercolours. I keep thinking I'll crash. That eventually, my body will take over and drag me under whether I want it to or not. That hasn't happened.

Sleep, it turns out, is petty - and I've apparently done something to piss it off.

This isn't new. I've never slept the way other people do , not the good kind. Not the soft kind that fixes you from the inside out.

Not the kind with dreams. I live in the liminal space between tired and unconscious. Where you're so close to falling you can feel your blood slow down, but some part of you refuses to let go.

I hover. I drift. I never land. My nights are a tightrope without an end, stretched over something I can't see, my toes curling just to keep balance.

Now it's worse. Sharper. Meaner. My thoughts spiral like they're trying to scrape something loose. My muscles ache in ways I can't stretch out. I exist in the in-between , that fogged-out place where everything is too loud, too bright, too much. The world feels like it's happening a room over, and I'm watching it through dirty glass.

I'm in the breakroom at work. It smells like burned coffee and the ghost of someone's reheated lasagne. The fluorescent lights buzz overhead, that low hum that only people like me can hear , the sleep-starved, the hyperaware, the almost-unravelled. Even the shadows in here are thin and twitchy, like they've been caffeinated too.

Jamie is talking. His voice is soft and low, which is exactly the wrong thing to do when I'm two blinks away from blackout. The gentler he is, the more I want to scream.

"…saw a sharp REM spike around the sixty-minute mark," he's saying. "Baseline dipped. Flatlined for almost ninety seconds."

I'm holding a pen above a clipboard like I might actually be participating. I am not. The form in front of me is blank. My eyes sting.

"Róisín?"

I blink. Slowly. My neck cracks when I turn to look at him.

He's wearing that look again, the one people use when they think you're about to fall apart, but they're too polite to say it out loud. Soft brow, half-frown, voice like he's handling glass.

"I'm fine," I say, before he can even ask.

He tilts his head. "You don't look fine."

"Thanks."

His mouth twitches like he might smile, but it doesn't land.

"You know you can go home. If you need to."

I nod. I don't move.

I won't go. We both know that. But it's a nice offer.

He stayed where he was, leaning against the counter, stirring his coffee like it had personally wronged him. "You've been pulling more night shifts than anyone else," he said, not looking up. "Don't think I haven't noticed."

I muttered something about the roster.

“Still,” he said, glancing at me now. “I’ve got admin visibility on all our logs. You’d be surprised what people miss when they think no one’s looking.”

He smiled like it was a joke. I didn’t laugh. I focus on the steam rising from his cup, the way it swirls like it’s trying to form letters before it disappears. For a second, I think I see my name in it. I blink and it’s gone.

By the time I leave, Galway’s bleeding rain.

The streets are slick with reflections, too bright, too sharp, too false. Headlights stretch like ghost-limbs across the pavement. Neon buzz flickers in every puddle. The sky hangs low and purple, bloated with weather it doesn’t know what to do with. The whole city smells like it’s been steeped in electricity, that sharp bite that makes your teeth ache if you breathe too deep.

I pull my hood low and walk fast, shoulders curled like I can disappear into my own coat.

The air smells like tarmac and chip grease and city salt, not sea salt, not the good kind. The kind that sticks to your clothes and makes everything feel clammy. The kind that says *you don’t belong here anymore.*

My boots slap through shallow gutters. I don’t bother avoiding them. Wet is wet.

The butcher's shop on the ground floor of my building is shut, but the stink is still there. Bleach and blood. That sick-sweet smell that clings to the walls and sinks into the grout. Like something once lived here and got scrubbed out too late. It's the kind of smell that sticks to your tongue, follows you upstairs, hides in your clothes.

The stairwell light sputters when I move past. Then dies.

Figures.

I climb in darkness. Two flights. Left turn. Third door. The key sticks, as always.

Inside, the flat greets me like a cold slap.

Not the dramatic kind. Not icy, cinematic cold. Just that deep, dead-in-the-walls cold that radiators can't touch. Old-building cold. The kind that wraps around your ankles and never let's go. It has a weight to it, like you could scoop it up in your hands and watch it pour through your fingers.

I don't turn the lights on. I don't need them. The shape of the place lives in my body now.

Bag down by the radiator. Coat off, fingers stiff. Shoes kicked toward the mat but never quite reaching it.

I move through the space like I'm retracing someone else's steps.

My flat isn't big. One bedroom, one bathroom with a mirror that turns you into a stranger if you stand there too long. The kitchen's not a room, it's a wall with ambitions. The fridge hums like it's self-soothing. The radiator wheezes like an asthmatic ghost.

It's cluttered, but clean. Familiar, if you squint.

Keys in the bowl. Mug in the sink. The blanket always rumpled, even when untouched. Everything where it should be, but nothing feels like mine.

It used to.

Now I feel like a squatter in my own life. Like the version of me who chose this place packed up weeks ago, left her skin behind, and forgot to warn the rest of me.

The kettle's already halfway full. It always is.

I move through the motions like a ghost haunting my own routine. Teabag. Mug. The kettle switch flicked. No thought required. My hands know what they're doing even if I don't.

Chamomile. I hate it. Always have.

It tastes like regret and dead flowers. It doesn't calm me, doesn't do anything. But I keep drinking it like maybe muscle memory can override biology. Like maybe if I go through the right sequence of motions, the ritual will trick my body into rest.

Tea equals comfort. Comfort equals sleep. Except it doesn't.

On the way back to the couch, I pass the hallway mirror.

It's already half-covered, scarf knotted loose in the corner, slipping just enough to show the edge of my face. I stop. Fix it. Pull the fabric down until all that's left is shadow.

Not because I'm superstitious.

Just... some nights, I can't look. Can't see the dull smear of my eyes. Can't track the curve of my mouth, drawn down and slack like it's forgotten how to lift.

I used to think mirrors were harmless. Then I watched my mother cover them, one by one, like they were windows left open in a storm. She never explained. Just said they "showed too much." Whispered while she cleaned them. Flinched if I played near one.

At the time, I thought she meant vanity. Now I'm not so sure.

There's something about mirrors that makes the air feel thinner. Like they're doors that remember how to open, even when you've forgotten how to knock. Too much depth in something that's meant to reflect. Too much space for something else to be looking back.

So I keep this one covered. Not for belief. Not really. Just because the habit stuck.
Because sometimes, it's easier not to know what's watching.

⋆⋆⋆

The kettle clicks behind me, sharp and final. I pour the water. Let the steam fog my glasses. My fingers drum against the side of the mug, a rhythm with no melody, just noise to keep the silence from settling in too deep.

The couch groans when I collapse into it. The blanket is rough, worn down at the seams. I pull it tight anyway. It smells like old detergent and nights I don't remember.

I tuck my legs beneath me. Hold the mug with both hands like it might anchor me to the floor. I sip. The tea burns my tongue.

Good. At least I can still feel something.

Above me, the ceiling waits.

There's a crack running along the plaster, just above the light fixture. It started as a thin hairline. Now it's growing. Like something beneath the surface is pushing downward, trying to get out. The edges seem darker tonight, as if something on the other side is pressed close.

I keep meaning to report it to the landlord. I never do. Tonight it looks different. Wider. Deeper.

I stare at it until my eyes sting. Half-daring it to fall. Half-wishing it would.

The flat is quiet. Not peaceful. Just still in that wrong kind of way, the kind that buzzes under your skin.

Nothing's out of place. Dishes done. Books stacked.

Curtains drawn. Window locked.

But the air is off.

The fridge clicks on. The radiator rattles once, then gives up.

I close my eyes. Just for a second. Not to sleep. I know better. Just to stop seeing.

When I open them, the mug is on the floor.

There's tea soaking into the rug. My fingers are empty. My mouth is dry. My heart is pounding like I've run five flights. My shirt clings to my back.

I don't remember letting go.

The blanket has slipped down my arms. My hip aches. My shoulder is twisted.

There was no dream. There never is.

Just that hum, soft and awful, like something brushed past. Like I missed a moment that almost happened. Like someone whispered my name through the floorboards, and I blinked too slow to catch it.

I sit up. Everything aches. My spine cracks. My hands shake. My breath stutters.

It feels like I've been *somewhere*. Somewhere I don't have words for.

I look up.

The crack in the ceiling has grown.

I tell myself I'll just sit there a minute, breathe until the thudding in my chest settles. My hands are still empty, fingers curling against the rough weave of the blanket. The tea stain on the rug spreads slowly, a pale brown bloom sinking into the fibres. I focus on that, on the shape of it, willing my head to stop spinning.

I blink.

And I'm standing.

Not in the flat, not anywhere. The floor beneath my bare feet is smooth as glass, but black, so black it swallows my toes when I look down. The air is a pressure, not a temperature, weightless and crushing at once, a silence so complete it fills my ears with the sound of my own heartbeat.

There's no colour here. No light except what catches the faint outlines of things that shouldn't exist.

To my left, the silhouette of a tree rises from the dark, its trunk and branches like carved obsidian, leaves frozen mid-rustle, edges catching a glint that isn't light so much as memory. To my right, a ripple in the air, suspended as if the moment of its movement had been trapped and hung there. Far ahead, an object floats chest-high, a porcelain cup, perfectly still, no tether, no shadow.

I try to move, but it's like wading through syrup. My breath sounds wrong. Muffled. The silence folds tighter, until it feels like it's listening.

A sound bleeds in, low, distant, layered. Not words yet, just tone. The shape of a voice. It curls around the edges of my name without quite forming it, breaking off halfway through as if it's been dragged under.

My chest tightens. I take a step toward the sound. Then another.

The black glass beneath me shows no reflection, but I feel something mirror the movement, an almost-step against my own, close enough to be felt in the bones.

"Hello?" My voice is a flat drop in a bottomless well.

The answer comes like a breath across the back of my neck, warm, deliberate. The layered voice strains to finish the word it almost said before.

Róis-

It stops.

The silence drops heavy again, sudden as a door slammed shut.

I spin, but the space is empty. The tree, the ripple, the floating cup, gone. The black glass stretches in every direction now, featureless.

Something shifts at my side. A warmth, fleeting, pressing briefly into the edge of me. Like a hand.

I suck in air-

- and I'm back on the couch.

The mug is still on the floor, tea still sinking into the rug. My chest is tight, my skin damp with sweat, a faint tremor in my arms. I lift a hand to my face and realise the scarf over the hallway mirror has slipped halfway down, its fabric fogged with a hand-shaped bloom of condensation, as if someone pressed their palm to it from the inside.

Chapter Two

Too Tired to Care

Róisín

I wasn't planning to go anywhere.

Didn't check the time. Didn't pick an outfit. Just found myself outside the flat, coat on, eyeliner smudged, hair tied back with the kind of effort that says I'm pretending. I didn't lock the door behind me. Didn't check the scarf on the mirror. Just needed to be somewhere the silence couldn't reach. My body moved like it already knew the route, like my hands and feet had agreed to this hours ago while my mind was still pacing the flat.

The pub wasn't my usual, if I even had a usual anymore. It was the kind of place where everything was dark on purpose, sticky floors, warm booths, a bar that smelled like spilled gin and cheap aftershave. Music loud enough to blur your thoughts. Voices layered thick over one another like insulation. I liked it. No one noticed you here unless you wanted them to. The walls were lined with crooked frames, black-and-white photos of fishermen and girls in big dresses, faces blurred enough that you couldn't quite tell if they were smiling or frowning.

I slid onto a stool at the corner of the bar and ordered a whiskey. Neat. The first sip was fire. The second was better. By the third, I'd remembered how to sit in my own skin without flinching.

He appeared somewhere in the blur between glass two and three.

Leaning against the bar like it owed him something, wearing a half-smile and a battered coat that looked like it had lived more lives than he had. Dark hair, ruffled like he'd been running his hands through it out of habit. The kind of face that reads warm in low light, but careful if you look too long.

"You don't look like someone who drinks whiskey for fun," he said, voice pitched low and dry.

I didn't bother looking at him. "Good. I'm not."

He laughed. Not mocking. Not surprised. Just... amused.

"Rough day?" he asked.

"Rough year," I said. "But who's counting."

He slid onto the stool beside mine like we'd already agreed to it. "What do you drink for, then?"

"Noise," I said. "It helps turn the volume down."

He tilted his head. “From what?”

I glanced at him then. Briefly. His eyes were kinder than I expected. “Everything,” I said. “My own brain, mostly.”

“Ah,” he said, like he understood. Like it wasn’t strange at all.

The slowest seconds passed.

“Want me to keep talking or shut up?” he asked.

That made me laugh, a real one, sharp and involuntary. “Talk. Just don’t ask questions you want honest answers to.”

“Deal.”

We talked.

About nothing important. About the songs on the playlist. About how every man over forty in the bar looked like he owned a boat and cheated on his wife. About how all the TVs played rugby even though no one was watching. I let my eyes wander over the crowd now and then, catching fragments, hands resting on knees that didn’t belong to their wives, someone mouthing the words to a song too quietly for anyone else to hear.

He told me he was between things. Work. Relationships. Definitions. Said his name was Adam. I didn’t give mine.

"You don't have to tell me who you are," he said after a while, like he could read the retreat coming before I made it.

"Good," I replied, and that was that.

I let my hand brush his when he passed me my drink. Let it linger half a second longer than it needed to. He smiled like he'd been waiting for that, not pushing, just open.

When he asked if I wanted to get out of there, I nodded before the question finished forming. It felt like deciding to step off a step without looking, small, dangerous, and over before I could change my mind

⋆⋆⋆⋆⋆⋆

His place was clean in that staged kind of way. Minimalist. Lived in only on weekends or when being alone got too loud. There was a leather couch that didn't look broken in. A coffee table that held nothing but a coaster and a single novel spine-down. The air smelled faintly of lemon cleaner, sharp and chemical, like he'd wiped the place down in a hurry before we left the pub

He handed me a glass of water. I took it, sipped once, set it down, and forgot it existed.

The kiss came quietly. No fireworks. No clumsy grab. Just two people looking to disappear into something that wasn't sleep.

I didn't want him. Not in the real way. But I needed something else to be inside for a while, something warm, something temporary. His hands were steady, his mouth tasting faintly of the whiskey we'd been trading like a secret.

Afterwards, he passed out beside me without a word.
I stayed awake. Of course I did.

There was a crack in his ceiling too. A faint line above the bed, branching like frostbite across the plaster. I stared at it until it started pulsing with my heartbeat. Like it knew I was watching.

I slipped out from under the blanket and dressed in silence. My skin felt too thin. My ribs too hollow.

In the bathroom, I splashed water on my face. There was a mirror over the sink. I didn't look. The air in the bathroom was still and heavy, like someone had been standing in front of that mirror for too long, breathing.

I left a note on the counter that said "Thanks." It felt stupid. Pointless. Like saying sorry after starting a fire.

⋆ ⋆ ⋆

The walk home felt longer than it should've. The city was quiet, caught in that breathless place between midnight and mourning. The streets shimmered under amber light, empty and wet. I walked fast. Every step echoed off the shopfronts like someone was keeping pace just far enough behind that I couldn't see them.

When I got inside, the scarf had fallen from the hallway mirror.

It was lying on the floor like it had been ripped down. Or maybe like it gave up holding back whatever was waiting behind the glass.

I didn't pick it up.

I stood in front of the mirror and stared at the reflection. For a moment, my own face felt unfamiliar, cheekbones sharper, mouth fixed in a shape I didn't recognise. And the reflection stared back, like it had been waiting all night for me to come home.

Chapter Three

Unseen

Taz

She doesn't dream. Not anymore.

But I feel her. Moving through the world like a ghost dressed in borrowed skin, sleep-starved and wired shut. I see her in the mirror's edge, in puddles dark with rain and light, in the soft frost crusting a bus window. Always blurred. Always slipping. But always there.

She is silence and static. And I am watching.

They think dreams are soft. Whispers. Vapour. No. Dreams are *teeth*. They bite. They drag. They remember. They get under the fingernails of your mind and stay there, lodged like splinters you can't dig out. They rot you slowly until you're mine again.

She was mine before she even knew what it meant to belong. Not lust. Not conquest. Something older than that. Older than language. Something written into the marrow before her first breath. Something carved in the wet clay of her soul when the world was still young enough to be changed by hands like mine. She crossed into my world barefoot, unafraid, starlight in her breath and dirt on her knees. We met in the unlit spaces. We built galaxies out of nothing. Named stars like secrets. She used to laugh in her sleep and I'd hold the sound like it might vanish if I let go.

And then she left.

No fight. No farewell. Just gone. She let them take her. Let them wipe the dark from her eyes and scrub the stars from her ribs. Let them poison her with logic. Wrap her in clinical sterility until the wild thing she was cracked and quieted.

She forgot me. Worse, she chose to.

Now she walks around in that fucking lab coat like it means something. Like it can shield her from what we were. From what I am. Like she can reason her way out of destiny.

But I remember. I always fucking remember.

I tried to reach her.

I gave her signs.

Carved symbols into the dreams of others. Flooded the sky with fire. Screamed into her skull until my voice broke on the walls she built around her mind.

She didn't flinch. Didn't blink. Didn't *listen*.

So now I wait.

And I rot. And I rage.

Every night is a cage and I am the animal pacing it, wearing the floor thin. I taste metal when I think of her, copper and salt and the memory of her name in my mouth.

Tonight, she slips into a bar that reeks of sweat and desperate men, and I follow her through the mirror behind the liquor bottles, fractured in bourbon glass and grease-streaked chrome. She orders whiskey. Neat. Her hand shakes, but her face doesn't betray her. She's learning to feel nothing. She's *getting good at it.*

And then *he* touches her.

I grind my jaw until my molars threaten to snap. He's nothing. Breath and borrowed confidence. Some forgettable shape wrapped in arrogance and aftershave. He says something cheap. She laughs like it's real. She touches his arm like it doesn't matter. Like she hasn't been touched in years and this is better than being alone.

I want to collapse the buildings around them. Instead, I memorise him. He'll dream soon. And I'll be waiting.

They walk. Her boots hit the wet pavement like defiance. He babbles, the kind of empty talk men use to fill silence. She doesn't hear him. She looks past him, past her reflection in the storefront glass. And for a breath, *a moment*, she sees me.

Just a flicker. A silhouette. The echo of something too familiar to ignore.

She blinks. Looks away and keeps walking.

“You fucking see me, Little Star!”

I roar it across every surface, through glass, metal, bone but her footsteps don’t falter.

She pretends it was nothing. Pretends I was never there.

His flat is soulless. Too clean. All straight lines and sharp corners, like a place that never expected company. He kisses her and she lets him. Not with hunger. Not with need. Just permission.

She moves like someone remote-controlling a body they forgot how to use. She doesn’t wince. Doesn’t tremble. Just folds into the moment like it might mean something if she stays still long enough.

It doesn’t.

He cums. She doesn’t. He doesn’t notice. But I do.

I catalogue every twitch, every shallow breath, the way her nails barely touch his skin as if even her touch is rationed now.

I watch the way her hand grips the sheet, not in ecstasy, but restraint. I see how her eyes drift past him to the ceiling, to the faint crack spidering outward like something alive.

She sees it. My mark.

I'm in every ceiling now. Every surface she hides beneath. My reach is longer than memory.

She breathes through her teeth when it's done. He rolls over. Spent. Snoring. She lies there, heart racing from nothing she asked for. Nothing she wanted.

She gets up. Runs the water in the bathroom. Doesn't look in the mirror. Not even once.

Fucking coward.

She leaves him a note. "Thanks." I spit at the word. Gratitude for *what*, Little Star? For letting your body be used like a room he forgot to lock on the way out?

By the time she reaches her own door, the scarf has fallen.

The one she hung like a boundary. A veil between us. A threadbare little spell she thought might keep me out.

It lies on the floor now, limp, discarded, like it gave up holding back the tide.

And she sees it. Freezes.

The fear rises fast. Raw. Unreasoned. It rolls off her in waves, not the kind shaped by logic, but the deep animal kind. The kind buried in the bones. The kind that whispers *run* before your mind knows why.

She sees me. Not a trick of the light. Not a shadow misread.

Me.

And by the Gods!, I see her. I see all of her.

The blood thrumming beneath her skin. The breath she forgets to take. The shimmer of sweat on her lip. That flicker behind her eyes like something just stirred, *mine*.

Recognition. Confusion. Terror. Desire.

It's faint. But it's there.

I press forward, closer to the glass. My hand against her reflection like I could tear straight through. My mouth inches from hers on the other side of the divide.

She flinches.

Good.

"You feel me now, don't you?" My voice is a growl, broken and dripping with want. "You fucking see me, Little Star."

The glass mists between us, my breath condensing over hers, a mingled fog that makes the moment look like it's already burning away.

She doesn't move. Doesn't breathe. Just stares, as if frozen in amber.

I want to drag her through the mirror and into me. I want to tear the walls down between us. I want to ruin her for anything that isn't *this*.

You forgot me.

But I never forgot you.

Not your voice in the dark. Not your pulse under my hands. Not the way you once curled into my chest like it was home.

They told you I was just a dream. A shadow. A lie you grew out of.

But I am not a story. And you are not safe.

I am real. And I am coming.

And no one, ***no one***, gets to touch what belongs to me.

Chapter Four

Breach
Róisín

I didn't sleep. Or maybe I did. But if I did, it wasn't the kind of sleep that comes with peace or silence or dreams that mean nothing. It felt instead like something passed through me in the dark, like the absence wasn't empty this time, but *occupied*, and whatever moved within it left its weight behind. It clung to me like damp clothes, as if I'd been walking through a fog no one else could see, and each breath still tasted of it.

The mirror had been uncovered when I woke. The scarf I always left draped over it, was usually pinned and secure, was lying crumpled on the floor, like it had been torn down in a hurry. I didn't remember touching it. Didn't remember looking into the glass. But the moment I saw it exposed, my skin turned to ice, and the shake in my hands started before I could rationalise it away. I had the sense of something caught mid-step, just outside my line of sight, waiting to see what I'd do

I told myself it was nothing, a stress reaction, a trick of perception, some half-baked illusion born from too many sleepless nights. I've written papers on what the mind does when pushed to the edge of exhaustion. I know the shape of hallucination. I've built an entire career out of understanding what most people dismiss. But even as I stood there staring at the steaming kettle, I realised I couldn't remember turning it on. I couldn't even remember entering the room.

The lab had that same wrongness, quiet in the way a room is quiet after a scream. A couple of the interns were out sick, and those who showed up moved slowly, like their bodies weren't properly attached to their minds. I clung to my normal, the morning checklist, equipment calibration, the cold safety of test logs. I needed sense, repetition, routine. Something to hold me steady.

Halfway through my second calibration check, I caught voices drifting from the archive room, not the usual low murmur of techs talking shop, but the brittle, half-nervous rhythm of people trying to laugh something off.

"…like it's saying something," one of them was saying. "Swear to God, slow the playback and you can hear it. Clear as day."

A chair scraped. Someone else chuckled, but it was the tight kind, the kind that doesn't touch the eyes. "Yeah? And what's it saying?"

There was a pause. "…Her name. I think."

I stood still in the corridor, pulse knocking at my throat. My first instinct was to step closer, but something in me recoiled, as if hearing my own name here would make it real.

The voices dipped, words blurring into the hum of the servers. A moment later, the taller of the two techs stepped into view, balancing a mug on top of a clipboard. He spotted me and straightened. "Morning, Roísín. Do you need the room?"

I shook my head before I'd even thought about it. "No. Just passing."

Back at my station, I stared at the log I'd been filling in, only to find the pen still moving. I didn't remember starting the spiral, but there it was, a tight, looping coil inked right across the margin. Not my usual quick, scribbled mess, but slow, deliberate lines like I'd been tracing the same shape for a very long time. The loops overlapped like ripples in water, hypnotic enough that I almost kept going just to see where they'd end.

I capped the pen. Pushed the clipboard aside. I tried to focus on the neat, sensible rows of data in front of me. But the hum in the walls felt heavier now, threaded with something almost tonal, like static that had learned the shape of my name.

It didn't last. Around mid-morning, the overhead lights in Room B flickered hard, like something was testing the power in short bursts. Then the EEG machine on Station 3 began spitting out irregular spikes so fast they looked like interference, they were jagged, erratic, pulsing with too much energy for Stage 2 sleep.

"Róisín?" Jamie's voice carried down the hall, edged with confusion. "You seeing this?"

I got up slowly, walked to the monitor, and stared at the brainwave data as if I might find an answer hidden in the noise. Patient 088's chart was unlike anything I'd seen - not in her file, not in anyone's. The curve was too steep, the frequency too fast. It wasn't sleep. It was *movement*.

"That's not... that's not a normal curve," I murmured, already knowing that was a useless understatement.

Jamie leaned in, rubbing at his jaw. "Either the leads are misfiring, or she's dreaming like she's sprinting through a war zone on coke."

I made a sound that might've been a laugh, but it caught partway up my throat and stayed there, thick and aching, because the shape of that wave was familiar. Not from the lab. From somewhere much closer. From the margins of my notebook - the ones I always assumed I filled during idle distraction, the ones I didn't remember writing at all.

"Did she flag anything in her intake?" I asked. "Recent trauma, medication changes, anxiety spikes?"

Jamie shook his head, already pulling up the file. "Nope. Clean. But she did say something weird when I was setting her up."

My stomach clenched. "Weird how?"

He shrugged, still distracted by the monitor. "Said she's been dreaming about someone following her. Said he had... *starry eyes*."

I went still. Not on the outside. But deep, somewhere under the ribs. My spine remembered something my brain couldn't reach - an image, or the ghost of one. A field. Pale light. A hand in mine. And eyes like space - wide and spiralling and ancient. Not a metaphor. Not poetry. *Galaxies.*

The memory didn't stay. It fractured and fell apart the moment I looked straight at it.

"Starry eyes," I echoed, like if I said it enough, it might make sense.

Jamie turned to look at me properly now, eyes narrowing in concern. "You alright? You look like you've -"

"I'm fine," I said, too fast. Too hard.

I turned before he could finish the sentence. I walked out of the room and didn't stop until the door to the supply closet was closed behind me and the darkness pressed against my eyes like a hand. I slid down the wall until I hit the floor, my pulse thundering in my throat. That phrase hadn't come from her. It hadn't even come from me recently. It came from somewhere *older*. Somewhere I can't remember.

The next moment fractured again. I blinked and found myself standing in the corridor outside Room D. I had no memory of walking there. No clipboard. Forty minutes missing from my day. I checked my watch. The numbers stared back at me like they were mocking the idea of normal time.

I drifted back to the front desk where Siobhán flagged me down about a print request I didn't remember. I told her it was sorted. I smiled. I played along.

But everything felt off-kilter - like the floor was slanted and no one else could feel it.

By the time I got home, I didn't feel tired. I felt *used up*. Carved out and left behind. The flat smelled like concrete and smoke and the bergamot candle I didn't remember lighting. I struck another match anyway, watched the flame take, watched the smoke curl. The smell reminded me of my mother, though I couldn't say why.

There was ash on the floor again, gathered beneath the mirror. I didn't look at the glass. I didn't ask questions. I swept it into the bin like it meant nothing. I don't know why I dug the box out. My mother's box. The one I kept in the back of the wardrobe like it might bite.

Beneath old scarves and brittle postcards, I found the book again. Not hers, older. Leather cracked like an old riverbed. The smell of dust and salt. I opened to a page near the middle, and the ink was so faded I had to tilt it into the lamp-light just to catch the words.

...The Oneiroi move in three... Morpheus shapes the story... Phantasos paints in glass, stone, and water... Ikelos feeds the fear... The rest bled into nothing, letters swallowed by time.

Lower down, I could just make out: *...must be given, not stolen... a mirror may open... the hand that bears the mark... the* *breach invites...* Then the ink blurred into an illegible black smear, as though someone had tried to rub the warning away.

I sat on the floor with my notebook and didn't think. Just let the pen move, my hand following lines I hadn't planned. Spirals. Slashes. The symbol from earlier - three jagged arms, looping and barbed. I'd drawn it already. I flipped back, found it again, over and over. The same shape I'd seen in 088's EEG.

I almost texted Jamie. But instead I shut the book.

I went to bed.

And this time, there was no drifting. No blur. No fade into static.

I *fell.*

The world was white. Not sterile - vast. Empty in the way a church is empty. High and echoing and full of waiting.

I stood in it, barefoot, blinking at a sky that didn't look like sky at all - curved, polished, perfect. A mirror that showed nothing. Not even me.

Then the crack came, sudden and clean, splitting the glass sky like it had always meant to break.

And through that crack, something entered.

I didn't need to see his face. The pressure changed the air. The gravity bent. The temperature dropped by ten degrees, and my bones knew him before my mind did.

He didn't move like a man. He moved like a concept - like something dreamt into shape. He raised his hand, not in greeting, not in anger, but with a slow and deliberate gesture, one finger extended toward me. Not toward my eyes. Toward my chest. As if he were pointing to something *inside* me. As if he were saying: *you already know*.

I gasped awake.

My skin was soaked. The sheets twisted like vines around my legs. I sat up too fast, chest heaving, eyes darting toward the ceiling.

The crack had grown. It split the plaster above me in a perfect mimicry of what I'd seen. And beneath it, drawn directly on the wall in what looked like ash, was the spiral.

I reached out. Pressed my palm to it.

It was still warm.

My phone buzzed from the nightstand. I reached for it with fingers that trembled like they weren't mine.

No number. No name.

Just one message:

You used to dream of me.

And even before I finished reading it, I already knew it was true.

Chapter Five

The Patient Who Screamed Her Name

Róisín

It started like any other session. Tuesday, dull as bone. The sky hung low and pale over Galway, misting the windows in the way that always made the lab feel slightly unreal, like we were floating somewhere above the real world, tethered only by routine. I hadn't slept. Not properly. My eyes burned and my teeth ached from clenching, but I moved through the morning like a body on strings, smiling at Siobhán, nodding at Jamie, reviewing the logs with hands that didn't feel like mine. Siobhán was eating toast at her desk, the kind that leaves butter stains on the paper beneath it, tapping her pen against her teeth as she scanned the intake forms. She asked if I wanted a slice. I said no, though the smell made my stomach turn in that restless, empty way that wasn't quite hunger.

The girl's name was Aisling. I noticed it when I pulled her file, and something in me clenched. A name like that doesn't belong in a place like this, too mythic, too pointed. It meant to dream. And yet she didn't look like a dreamer. She looked thin and stretched and quietly worn, her skin too pale for August, her hair braided neatly like someone had done it for her. Her eyes were soft, but not fragile. The kind of softness that came from restraint, not weakness. I caught myself wondering who plaited it, mother, sister, carer? The neatness of it felt like someone else's hand, the same way her cardigan looked borrowed, sleeves hanging past her wrists.

She didn't speak much. Signed her forms. Lay back. Let me fit the electrodes with the kind of stillness I usually only see in patients who've done this before, the long-haul ones. Trauma studies. Sleep deprivation trials. The broken ones. Her pulse was steady under my fingers when I adjusted the sensors, but there was a tightness there, like a note held too long.

We weren't running anything complex, just a controlled descent for pattern observation. Mid-depth sedation. Nothing invasive. Nothing risky. A session meant to give us a clean window into her REM profile.

I remember noting how smooth the transition was. Her waves fell like silk, no spikes, no delays. It was beautiful, in a clinical way. Something that made sense.

Until it didn't.

The first spike came at thirteen minutes in. A blip, sharp and abrupt, cleaving straight through theta like a scream through glass. I blinked. Stared at the waveform. Rechecked the lines. It wasn't a fault. It wasn't equipment.

"Jamie," I called, but not loud enough for him to hear. I stayed seated. Watched.

Her breathing shifted. Shallow, but regular. Her eyes were moving beneath the lids, fast. Too fast. It wasn't the erratic twitch of dreaming. It was frantic. Purposeful. Like she was searching for something.

And then she said my name.

Not loudly. Not like a warning. Just… a whisper. A brush of sound shaped like me.

"Róisín," she breathed.

I stood. The monitor glowed quietly behind her, full of lines I couldn't explain. Seven seconds. Full amplitude. Not seizure. Not sleep-talking. Something else.

"Róisín," she said again, louder.

Her mouth shaped it with intent. Like she meant it. Like she knew it.

I stepped back. My throat closed around nothing.

The EEG trembled.

She said it a third time, and then she screamed.

Not a cry. Not a startled noise. A scream from the gut, tearing through her body with such force her back arched off the bed. Her limbs seized. The lights overhead flickered. The monitor exploded into static.

"Róisín!"

It didn't sound like her voice anymore.

Jamie crashed through the door. "What the fuck?"

The scream cut off.

Aisling went limp.

The static cleared. The waveform flatlined into normalcy, like nothing had happened. Like the room hadn't just tried to break in half.

We both stared at the screen.

Jamie broke the silence first. "That wasn't a night terror."

"No," I said. My voice felt distant. Like it didn't want to belong to me.

"She screamed your name."

"I know."

He looked at me. Really looked. "Did you do something?"

That made me blink. "What?"

He held up his hands. "I mean, not like that. Just… did she know you before this? Did you speak to her about any-?"

“No,” I said. Too fast.

She woke up five minutes later like nothing had happened. Told us she’d dreamt of a house on fire. Said she remembered someone calling from the other side of the wall. She didn’t remember screaming. Didn’t remember my name. She asked for water in a voice that sounded like it had been scraped thin, and when I passed her the cup, her fingers brushed mine like she was trying to check if I was real.

I made her sit in observation longer than necessary. Jamie hovered nearby, watching me from under his lashes like he didn’t know if I might detonate too.

Eventually, we let her go.

The lab felt heavier without her in it, like she’d left a pressure behind that clung to the air vents and corners. I stayed in the control room, watching the closed feed even after Jamie powered down the main monitor. The last freeze-frame of her face lingered on the smaller screen in front of me, mouth slack, lashes trembling against her cheeks as if she were still listening for something.

The footage should have ended there. It didn’t.

Somewhere between rewinding and pausing, the room in the video stuttered, one flicker, no more than half a second, and the background behind Aisling shifted. The pale wall and cabinet blurred into something darker, edges jagged, light pooling low to the ground like water.

When it snapped back, she was still there, still asleep, but my own name was written in the margin of the EEG printout on the desk beside her. I didn't remember putting it there.

My hand was still clutching the pen when Jamie reappeared, holding a stack of forms. He hesitated in the doorway. "You've been sitting there for forty minutes."

"I was reviewing," I said, though when I looked down, the notes in front of me weren't notes at all. Line after line of spirals, the same tight coil Aisling's brainwaves had formed before she screamed. I tore the page out and stuffed it into the pocket of my lab coat without meeting his eyes.

On my way out, I cut through the corridor that passed the observation glass. For a heartbeat, my own reflection was there, lagging half a step behind. The figure in the glass had her mouth open like she was speaking, but the hallway was silent. Her lips shaped a word I couldn't hear but recognised by the way it pulled something in my chest tight.

I didn't stop to see what she'd said.

By the time I made it home, I felt like I'd been carrying something for hours without realising it. My spine ached. My ribs hurt. My brain had too many doors open.

I didn't light a candle. Didn't put the kettle on. Didn't check the mirror.

I lay on the couch, clothes still on, heartbeat too loud in my ears.

And sleep came.

Not slow. Not kind.

It took me like a riptide.

And this time, I didn’t float.

I fell.

Chapter Six

The Mirror Room
Róisín

I knew it was a dream the moment I felt the silence.
Not the muted quiet of the city at four in the morning, when traffic is nothing but a distant hum and the radiator ticks like an impatient clock, but a silence that had weight. A silence so absolute it pressed against my eardrums like deep water.
It hummed under my skin, a low frequency my bones seemed to recognise, something older than the flat, older than me.

I was standing in white. The ground under my feet wasn't marble, it wasn't tile, it was too smooth, too seamless, cool without being cold. It gave slightly under my toes, not like stone, but like something alive pretending to be stone. The air didn't shift. The space above wasn't a sky at all, but a perfect, unbroken dome curving high overhead like the inside of a vast, empty shell.

And all around me, mirrors.

They weren't placed with any sense of order. They rose from the ground like monuments to something long-forgotten, tall, fractured, leaning, flawless. Some towered over me like sentinels, others stood at angles as if they'd been moved and abandoned mid-thought. Every surface gleamed with a strange, liquid clarity, yet showed nothing. No reflection. No light. Just darkness lurking on the other side, like a corridor waiting for someone to step through.

The air around them felt colder, as though each one bled its own weather into the room. Some smelled faintly of saltwater, that clinging tang that makes you feel damp to the bone. Others carried a dry, metallic scent like old coins pressed against the tongue. I thought I heard wind once, but it was only the faint shift of breath between two mirrors I wasn't standing nearby.

I didn't move. I didn't breathe. The stillness here wasn't empty. It was expectant, like the moment before a curtain lifts.

I glanced down; my feet were bare. I couldn't remember if they had always been. The skin of my soles prickled, as if the floor was aware of me standing on it.

When I finally turned, one of the mirrors held my reflection. But it wasn't right.

I was there, yes, but I wasn't in control. The reflection tilted her head first. Slowly. Like she was studying me the way you might watch an animal to see if it bites. And then she smiled.

It wasn't cruel. But it wasn't kind either. It was the kind of smile that said she knew something I didn't and wasn't going to tell me unless it served her.

I stepped back. The reflection didn't.

A sound moved through the space. Not loud. Just a breath. Low and deliberate, as if it came from behind the glass.

The mirrors stretched endlessly in every direction. I began to walk, slow and cautious. In each surface I passed, something flickered: a glimpse of my childhood bedroom; the hum of the lab; my mother's turned face, hair falling like a curtain to hide her expression. None of them stayed for more than a heartbeat.

In one, I saw the spiral, my spiral, drawn over and over in black ash. In another, a house burning quietly, the flames bending inward as though breathing. Somewhere far down the line, I caught the pale glint of salt scattered across a dark floor.

Then I saw him.

Far down the row, caught in the edge of a tall, narrow mirror set slightly askew, a figure. A man.

He didn't move. Didn't lean closer. Just watched. I couldn't see his face. The shape of him was there, tall, broad shoulders, dark hair, but every time my gaze tried to settle on the details, they slipped away like water through my fingers. I knew that absence. Knew the shape of what I wasn't seeing.

Something in my chest tightened.

I took a step toward him. And another. Each one felt heavier than the last, as though the air had thickened to syrup. My calves ached like I'd been wading for hours. I kept my eyes on him, afraid that if I looked away for even a second, he would be gone.

And then, he was. The mirror stood empty.

But the breath was closer now.

I felt it on the back of my neck. Warm, steady, deliberate. I turned, and he was there.

Not in a mirror. Not watching from a distance. Here. In the space with me. I hadn't heard him move. Hadn't felt a footstep. He was simply there, close enough that the air between us belonged to him.

The dome above and the ground below seemed to tilt toward him, a slow bow.

My pulse stuttered against my throat. The air felt different around him, heavy in a way that bent inward, like gravity shifting toward a black star.

I couldn't move. Couldn't speak. My mouth was dry.

He didn't touch me. Didn't whisper. But the weight of his presence slid down my spine like a hand. Not gentle. Not unkind. Just… inevitable. My body reacted before my mind caught up, a tightening low in my stomach, a shiver that had nothing to do with fear, though fear was threaded through it.

He leaned closer. Close enough that my hair stirred without wind. I felt the faintest pressure at the crown of my head, like he was reading something written in me.

And then he spoke.

"You've been here before."

It wasn't a question.

My throat tried to shape words, but nothing came out.

His eyes, I didn't see them, but I knew they were there, fixed on me like pins through paper.

"You left me," he said, voice layered and strange, as if spoken through two mouths at once. "But you keep my mark."

The spirals. The crack. The ash. They weren't following me. They were his.

My breath came shallow. "Who are you?" I managed.

His mouth didn't move. The answer pressed into the air between us like a hand on glass. "You already know."

For a heartbeat, the mirrors behind him lit, not with light, but with movement. Thousands of reflections that weren't mine. Places I'd never been. Skies I'd never seen. All of them shifting like cards in a shuffling deck, and in each, his shadow somewhere near.

Before I could take a step, he reached past me. Not touching, just letting his hand hover by my side, and the nearest mirror flared with colour. Blue so deep it hurt. The reflection in it stepped forward.

It was me. But older. Or maybe younger. Or maybe not me at all. She pressed her palm to the glass.

I felt heat in my own hand before I realised, I'd mirrored her.

The moment my skin met the surface, the white dome split with a sound like breaking bone.

And I woke.

The dark in my flat felt wrong, too thick. My breath was fogging the window glass, even though the heat was on. My body still remembered the weight of him, the heat of him.

The scarf was still over the mirror.

I didn't check it. Because I knew, without needing to look, he might still be there.

And when I pulled my hand from under the blanket, the spiral was faintly visible across my palm in ash.

Chapter Seven

The Absence

Taz

She stepped through, and the dreamworld exhaled for the first time in years.

The moment her presence crossed the threshold, my realm shifted. Pressure built like a tide against a cliff, then broke, flooding every surface, every shadow. The white plain beneath her feet rippled once, as if tasting her weight. The mirrors shuddered in their frames, a thousand still mouths whispering in a language that belonged only to us.

Every corner of this place recognised her, not as an intruder, but as the one absence it had been built to grieve. The dome above swelled with a low resonance, the kind that hums in bone marrow and teeth, until the whole realm seemed to bow to her return.

Even the void leaned forward.

She had not dreamed in years. Not truly. Not in a way that could bring her here, to the locked places I keep behind the eyes of lesser minds. She'd drifted on the edges, weightless, formless, brushing my borders like a ghost in her own skin. But this… this was flesh and heat and pulse.

I had broken her famine.

It did not feel like joy. It did not feel like relief. It felt like the slow, exact pull of an arrow freed from the string after decades of holding. Triumph, yes, but triumph gone half-feral from starvation. The years I had whispered into her absence, the spirals I had carved into her waking walls, the cracks I had widened in her ceiling, all threads leading here, to the moment her bare feet touched my ground.

She appeared as she once did, and yet not at all. There was no child in her now, no unshaped innocence. Only a woman who had been tempered in the fire of her own resistance yet still carried the echo of what she had been with me. Her movements were wary, yes, but they drew the air with them, bending the space in quiet devotion.

I did not go to her. Not immediately. I let the mirrors greet her first.

They remembered her palms from before, the heat of her skin pressed to glass, the way her fingertips had once dragged across their surface as though testing the thinness of the divide. They showed her fragments the waking world had buried under logic and grief: her mother's profile turned away, the narrow bed where she first slept in my arms, the salt-dark horizon we once stood beneath. Each time the visions dissolved, I felt the pulse in her throat falter. Her body recognised the loss even if her mind still pretended not to.

And Gods, the way she moved.

Every line of her was an unintentional prayer. The set of her shoulders, the arch of her spine, the curve of her mouth, all tempered by exhaustion that had calcified into habit. She was not delicate; she was unbreakable in the way of things that have already been broken and reforged. The scar along her jaw, the birthmark on her hip, the shadow-worn skin beneath her eyes, these were my marks too, though she did not yet understand it.

Then it happened.

She felt me.

Not in thought. Not in the part of her that insists on order and evidence. She felt me in the old places, in the marrow, in the blood still carrying my imprint from when she slept and woke in my keeping. Her breath betrayed her first, quickened, caught between caution and want. Then her spine locked, not in defence, but in that ancient surrender her body had never forgotten.

I was behind her without movement, without sound. The space itself curved to allow it.

Her warmth reached me first, that particular heat that belongs only to the living. Then her scent, rainwater, skin, the faint ghost of fabric against her body, and beneath that, something I recognised as mine, though it had lain dormant for years.

My cock ached at the nearness of her, not with the shallow hunger of a passing urge, but with the deep, claiming need of something vital returned to me.

Her skin gave her away before her voice could. Goosebumps blossomed along her arms. Nipples tightened against thin cotton. Her thighs pressed subtly together, the smallest motion, but I saw it. Felt it. Every involuntary shift was a confession, every quickened breath an invocation.

I could have taken her then. Could have set my hand at her hip, drawn her back into me, reminded her of every way she'd bent for me before. But not yet.

This was resurrection. I would not waste it on haste.

She opened her mouth, the dream swallowed the sound, swallowing it into the white. It didn't matter. Her body told me what she meant. The slight lean, the angle of her hips, the stillness threaded with surrender, she remembered. Not with her mind. With her bones.

I let my breath drift over the curve of her shoulder, no touch, no claim, just the weight of inevitability. Her body went taut, and the sound she made, low and unbidden, almost undid me entirely.

The realm felt it too.

The mirrors nearest to us pivoted with a slow groan, turning their faces inward like hounds circling prey. Her reflection, the one directly ahead, stopped mimicking her movements and began moving on its own, tilting its head to me instead of her. I let it. Let her see her own face offer me a smile she didn't know she could make anymore.

The ground beneath her feet softened, not to trap, not yet, but to remind her it could.

The breach was open.

The walls between us were crumbling, hairline fractures widening with every breath she took in my air. The spiral turned again, slow and unstoppable. Tomorrow she will run her little tests and find my imprint tangled in her data. She will hear my name on other lips. She will feel it tighten around her ribs, coil low in her belly, the way she once did when she whispered it into my chest.

Taz.

When she remembers fully, when she comes not out of instinct but choice, eyes steady, hands unflinching, I will take her back into the depths she abandoned.

And I will keep her there until she forgets waking ever existed.

Chapter Eight

When the Wall Breaks

Róisín

I woke wet.

Not the dampness of a fever, not the sweat trapped under too many blankets. This was deeper. Slick between my thighs, sheets sticking to me as though they'd been wrapped tight around heat and friction until the moment my eyes opened. The air was cool now, but my skin was still flushed in places that had forgotten how to blush. My chest ached; my nipples were peaked and tight under the thin cotton of my shirt. My breath was shallow, uneven, not the rhythm of someone waking from a nightmare. No. This was the aftermath of something slower.

I lay still, staring into the dark. Waiting for the dream to dissolve the way they always did. It didn't. It stayed. Sharp at the edges.

White. Endless, horizonless white. A forest of mirrors rising like monuments. And him.

Not touching. Not speaking. Just there. Close enough for the air to bend around him, close enough for my body to betray me before my mind could catch up. The heat of him grazing the back of my neck. That stillness that wasn't stillness at all, it was focus, absolute and crushing, like gravity deciding I was worth its full attention.

Mine.

I remembered the way my hips had shifted without my permission. The shiver running my spine like a live current. The uncoiling want in a body that had been untouched in every way that mattered for too long. And how, in the mirror nearest me, my reflection stopped being mine at all.

You remember me.

My hand slid down, almost without thought. I flinched at the sensitivity, the rawness, at the proof that what had happened had weight beyond sleep. I'd been wanting, aching. Not in the distant, hazy way of fantasy, but in the here-and-now ache of the real.

And the worst part? It hadn't felt imagined. It had felt like him.

The window was fogged from the inside. A single smudge at its centre. Not random, not the scatter of a passing hand, but deliberate, oval-shaped, as if someone had leaned in and breathed against the glass from the other side. I told myself it was mine. My breath. My heat. My nonsense.

I'm closer than you think.

I didn't touch it.

The phone buzzed once. No text. A missed call. Fiadh.

The sight of her name made something tighten low in my stomach. We didn't talk like that. If she needed me, it was quick, perfunctory, usually through Dad.

One voicemail.

I pressed play.

"Róisín." Her voice was sharper than I remembered it ever being, words clipped, caught between breaths. In the background, wind? No, too steady. Like a radio tuned between stations. A hiss and crackle that made my teeth hurt. She dropped her voice, muffled, as though turning away from the phone. "Cover the mirror."

A pause. Muffled conversation, not with me. Then back to her, faster now, urgent: "Don't wait. It's already watching."

The message cut off.

I sat there with the phone still in my hand, the sheets cooling around me, the metallic tang of the dream still in my mouth. Fiadh didn't panic. Not in front of me. Not ever.

Eventually, I pushed myself up. The towel I'd left by the bed slid to the floor.

The bathroom mirror caught me before I was ready. Steam still clung faintly to the glass from the water I'd run hours earlier. My reflection was blurred, soft at the edges, but when I tilted my head, she didn't move with me. Half a beat behind. Just enough to notice. Just enough to make me step back.

I turned away before she could catch up.

In the kitchen, I stood by the kettle without turning it on. My eyes fixed on the blank wall above the counter. Somewhere in the back of my mind, the dream shifted, not the mirrors this time. A black expanse. Still water. And above it, a crown of stars in a perfect circle, drifting as though it were looking for the head it belonged to.

I blinked, and it was gone. The fridge clicked on. My phone screen was black again.

The lab felt wrong.

Too bright. Too quiet. The overhead lights seemed harsher, bleaching the edges of things. Everyone else moved like nothing had shifted, but my skin felt over-aware, every inch of me humming from the dream. I kept catching myself wanting to close my eyes, to see if I could slip back into that white.

You could.

We passed in the narrow corridor. Jamie stepped aside just enough for me to squeeze past, but not enough to make it easy. "You've got that far-away look again," he said.

"Lack of sleep," I muttered.

"Mmm." His eyes stayed on mine, too sharp for casual. "You were never supposed to wake like this, you know."

I stopped, but he was already walking away.

⋆ ⋆ ⋆

When I finally pulled up my personal sleep tracker, my throat tightened.

The usual flatline was gone.

In its place, a clean descent into Stage 2. A hard REM spike, twenty-four minutes in, sustained and irregular with multiple bursts.

Impossible.

Seventeen years of silence. And now this.

I did that.

It was my data. My brain. My dream.

I closed the file before my hands could shake harder.

"Bad curry?" Jamie called from the breakroom.

"Bad reality," I muttered, and kept walking.

Aisling's log was still open on my desktop, waiting. The spirals were there, neat this time, clean, deliberate. The same spirals I'd started sketching in my journal without knowing why. Shapes I shouldn't know, but my hand remembered them.

Jamie reappeared, leaning around the divider. "Room D had a weird one last night. Simmons muttered something in his sleep. Sounded like 'Taz.' Or maybe 'toss.' Thought you'd want to flag it."

Taz.

The name landed low, sharp and certain. It didn't belong to me, but it knew me. My pulse stuttered.

"What was the tone?" I asked.

Jamie frowned. "Like it hurt to say."

Good.

I listened to the audio alone. Simmons breathing slow, the faint shift of sheets, then the word, dragged out, cracked in the middle.

Ta-z…

I ripped the headphones off. My palms were slick. I didn't know that name. And yet… I did.

Say it.

I went home early.

The long way. Rain had rinsed the city raw, leaving the streets slick and shining. Shopfronts glowed in puddles, colours stretched long and unreal. I walked fast, hood low, letting the rhythm of my boots on wet tarmac try to scrape the inside of my head clean. But every glass surface, bus shelters, shop windows, even the shallow skin of rainwater pooled in potholes, felt like an open eye.

By the time I reached the flat, the candle wouldn't light. The scarf still hung over the mirror, heavy with meaning I wasn't ready to test.

I sat with my journal, meaning to write clinical notes. The pen didn't listen.

It wrote his name instead, over and over.

Taz.

Taz.

Taz.

Perfect.

Between each one, the spiral. Neat now. Exact. Balanced.

I pressed my finger to the centre.

The paper was warm.

Chapter Nine

Reflections

Róisín

I didn't sleep.

Not because I couldn't, but because closing my eyes felt like handing over the keys to a house I wasn't sure I'd get back. Every time I even thought about drifting, I felt him there. That weight pressed against my back, the impossible heat on the nape of my neck, my body's betrayal, answering without permission, waking slick and aching in places that had been dormant for years.

I'd pressed a pillow between my thighs just to still the pulse. It hadn't helped. If anything, it made me more aware of it. The wanting. The sharp, uninvited ache that didn't belong to a dream at all.

I made it to the lab on autopilot, hands buried deep in my sleeves so no one could see the tremor.

The corridor lights flickered when I swiped my pass. Not the lazy flutter of faulty wiring, no, this was a slow, deliberate stutter, a pause in illumination that made the air between me and the far wall feel too long. My skin prickled as if something had just walked past.

Jamie caught me halfway down the hall.
"Jesus, Ro. You look… not great."

"Thanks. Very clinical of you."

He didn't laugh. Just tilted his head, eyes flicking over me like he was scanning for data. "You sure you're okay?"

"I didn't sleep. That's all."

"You've said that every day this week."

"Then you should be used to it."

I moved to pass him, but his hand brushed my arm. Not hard. Just enough to register.
"If you ever want to talk," he said, quieter now, "off the record… I'd listen."

It wasn't the words that caught me. It was the way they lingered, low and warm, like he was holding them out and waiting for me to take them. Something I didn't trust myself to step toward.

Later, I stood at the bathroom sink, splashing water over my face, trying to wash off whatever invisible residue clung to me. The fluorescent light hummed overhead, sharp against the tiles. I looked up.

And he was there.

Not a flicker. Not a trick of my peripheral vision. A man. Bare-chested. Shadow-eyed. Fixed on me through the mirror with the kind of stillness that makes your body understand possession before your mind catches up.

Every part of me locked. My lungs forgot their work. My pulse slammed against my ribs.

I turned.

Nothing.

The mirror reflected only me again, pale, damp-haired, but the imprint of him still pressed from the inside of my skin like a bruise.

I didn't last the day. Told Siobhán I felt off, which wasn't a lie, and left.

By the time I got home, I was peeling clothes from my body in the hallway. The air in the flat felt thick. Heavy.

The shower hissed to life, water coming down hard and scalding. Steam filled the glass before I'd even stepped in. I wanted the heat to burn something clean into me.

I tilted my head back, eyes closed, letting the spray run over my face until the world narrowed to heat and heartbeat.

And then -

Hands.

Not mine.

Fingertips grazing the slope of my waist, sliding up to the sides of my ribs. Strong palms locking around my hips, steadying me, grounding me, claiming me.

I gasped, eyes snapping open, but the only thing in the room was the glass.

Only, it wasn't *just* glass anymore.

Through the veil of steam, he was there. Not in the room. Not physically. But present. Leaning in from the other side of the pane with a smirk that was all claim and certainty, the kind of expression that says: *I've already taken you, and you haven't even realised it yet.*

My breath came fast. My hand moved without thought, sliding between my thighs, fingers parting slick heat. I shouldn't have, but my body already knew the language. It remembered the tilt of my hips, the pace, the surrender.

The water beat against my skin, but all I felt were his hands, firm on my hips, one sliding around to rest just under my ribs, the other curling loosely at my throat. Not cruel. Not tentative. Just holding me in place like every inch was his.

A sound broke from me, sharp and breathless.

Then his voice filled the space between my ear and my bones, velvet over dark iron.

"I'd burn constellations just to be near you. Say the word, Little Star, and I'll carve your name into the sky and set the rest of it on fire."

My knees almost gave out. My fingers moved faster. The pressure built sharp and unbearable.

"You used to beg for me in sleep," he murmured, low and dangerous. "All I'm asking now is for you to remember."

I came hard. My whole body clenched and shook, forehead pressed to the tile as the spray blurred the edges of the world.

"My Goddess."

The words didn't just land, they exploded. Reverberated through every nerve, like they'd been lying in wait for years.

And then -

Gone.

The hands. The voice. The heat.

Only the steam remained.

⋆ ⋆ ⋆

I stayed braced against the wall, thighs trembling, heart hammering in my chest. My breath came in shallow pulls.

I didn't know if I was being haunted or hunted.

And I didn't know if I wanted to be saved.

But I knew one thing with terrifying clarity.

I didn't want him to stop.

Chapter Ten

Breach lines

Taz

She saw me today.

Not the flicker of a shadow, not the afterimage of a blink. She *saw* me, clearly, deliberately, in the lab bathroom, beneath that thin strip of light that hummed like a dying star. She stared into me, and for a breath, she forgot to breathe at all. Her pupils blew wide, her pulse spiked, and the shape of her body told me everything I needed to know.

That moment was mine.

I stretched it until the air between us felt like a thread pulled taut enough to cut skin. Then I left. Not to hide, I don't *hide*, but to sink the hook deeper. To make her carry me through her day like an infection in the bloodstream.

And she did.

I stayed close.

In the curve of chrome faucets, in the ripple of black coffee in her cup, in the gloss of a monitor screen she didn't remember checking twice. Watching. Listening. Feeling her nerves fray one fine strand at a time. Every time she blinked, I was there, ready to step in if she lingered too long.

Jamie touched her.

A nothing gesture to him, a brush of his hand against her arm in the corridor, but to me, it was a trespass. Her soul flinched even if her face didn't show it. He thinks of himself as harmless, the quiet one, the patient one. The man who waits at the edge of her exhaustion, lowering his voice and leaning close like patience is a form of care.

But I've walked through his dreams.

★ ★ ★

He cornered her outside the records room. It looked casual, the kind of half-smile, half-step closer that reads like coincidence to anyone not paying attention, but he blocked the narrow space with his body, subtle as a lock clicking shut.

Her back brushed the cold wall. He held a file between them like an offering, his fingers grazing her wrist when she reached for it. Not clumsy. Not accidental. Intent wrapped in politeness; the kind you can't call out without being made to feel paranoid.

She froze. She didn't pull back, but she didn't step forward either. The smile she gave him was a tool, one she'd used before, the kind that slips you out of a tight space without a scene.

I was in the glass of the door behind him, a shadow among shadows.

He glanced over his shoulder. His eyes caught me.

For a heartbeat, he couldn't decide if I was a trick of light or a threat. The instinct was there, the way his breath caught, the way the colour drained just enough for me to notice. His gaze snapped to her, then back to the reflection, searching for a shift, a giveaway.

I didn't move.

I held his stare until his fingers whitened on the file. She murmured something soft, meaningless, and slid past him. He turned to watch her leave.

I was still there. Not smiling. Not blinking.

He left quickly.

* * * * *

Jamie is rotted underneath. He doesn't want her safe. He doesn't want her loved. He wants her unravelled, piece by piece, until she leans on him out of need rather than choice. He wants to be the one she collapses in front of, so he can mistake ownership for intimacy.

But she is not his to catch.

She is mine.

And if he tries to take what's mine, I will open him from the inside out.

Later, in the steam, she let herself go.

She doesn't understand that I'm not bound by time. I don't have to wait for her to call my name. All she has to do is *want*, and I am there.

The moment she stepped under the water, I pressed into the space around her. The glass fogged, but I kept my shape visible, the slope of my shoulders, the cut of my jaw, the stillness she's already started to crave. I wanted her eyes to widen. I wanted her thighs to press together before she even touched herself.

When she did, when her fingers slid between her legs, I felt it like a current running through me.

I wrapped myself around her wrist. Not to stop her. To guide her. My phantom hands traced her ribs, her breasts, down to where her need was sharpest. My palm cupped her throat, not to choke, but to anchor her to the moment. To *me*.

The words I gave her weren't just for arousal. They were a key. A memory. A truth buried so deep she's forgotten the taste of it.

I told her I'd burn constellations for her. That I'd carve her name into the dream-sky and set the rest ablaze. Once, I had. Once, the whole horizon had burned in her honour, and she'd laughed in my arms like she had no idea how to be afraid.

Her hips answered me now as they had then, instinct first, thought second. The sound she made was mine.

I could have stepped through. I could have shattered her resistance tonight and taken her fully. But not yet.

I want her desperate.

I want her begging.

When she came, it was half-sob, half-offering, her body bowing forward as if trying to meet me through the glass.

Break for me, Burn for me, my Goddess.

The truth sank into her bones.

She slumped against the tile, trembling, wrecked, alone.

But never untouched.

Chapter Eleven

The Forest of Breathing Trees

Róisín

I knew I was dreaming the moment the trees inhaled.

It wasn't wind that moved them. They swelled, *expanded*, their pale trunks stretching like ribs under skin, silver light rippling along their lengths. Branches curled inward on the exhale, slow, deliberate, then unfurled toward the bruise-coloured sky on the inhale, skeletal fingers flexing in time with a heartbeat I couldn't place.

The sound wasn't rustling. It was whispering. Thousands of voices murmuring in a language I didn't know, a thread of secrets passed leaf to leaf, trunk to trunk.

The ground gave under my bare feet, not moss, not earth, something warmer. Springy. The absurd thought came that I was standing on skin, and the longer I stayed still, the more I could *feel* it… the faintest pulse beneath the surface, syncing with my own.

The air smelled wrong. Rich, wet earth, yes, but laced with something acrid and sweet, like the breath from a locked drawer opened after decades.

I stood in a clearing ringed by breath. The perimeter shifted with each inhale and exhale, the forest closing in, then retreating.

"This isn't real," I whispered, because naming a thing is supposed to make it smaller. "You're not real."

I closed my eyes. Opened them again.

The forest remained.

The trees exhaled.

And then I heard it.

My name.

Not spoken like human speech, but poured, low, liquid, older than anything that should know how to shape my syllables.

Róisín.

I turned.

He was half in shadow, but the dark didn't hide him. Bare-chested, barefoot, the breadth of his shoulders cutting through the air like a blade. His eyes weren't eyes at all. They were constellations collapsing inward, spirals of stars and dust, gravity made visible and aimed entirely at me.

"You're not real," I said again, louder, as though the volume could make it true.

He took one step forward. The space between us changed temperature.

"This is a dream," I pushed, my voice sharp. "I'm asleep in my flat, and I'm… I'm losing it. This is lucid-looping, stress-induced… sleep-dep psychosis. I've *written* papers on this."

His mouth curved. "Then you," he said, voice carrying without effort, "should know how fragile reality really is."

I took a step back, though the ground swallowed the sound of it. "Get out of my head."

"I never left."

The words sank into me, threading through the tightness in my ribs. His gaze locked on mine, not cruel, not kind, but inevitable.

"You used to dream of me."

I shook my head. "No."

He tilted his head, studying me like a rare animal that might still bite. "You called me by name."

"I don't know your name."

"You said it in the shower."

The blood drained from my face. The trees around us rippled like disturbed water.

He stepped forward again, not chasing, just closing. The forest seemed to lean with him.

"You're not real," I tried again, but my voice was breaking now.

"Then wake up."

I squeezed my eyes shut, bracing for my flat, the broken heater, the flickering kettle, the scarf over the mirror.

When I opened them, he was closer.

The trees had gone still. The whispering had stopped. The air was thick enough to taste, metallic and warm, as though the forest itself was holding its breath for my answer.

"I don't want this," I said, but the crack in my voice told the truth for me.

His expression shifted, not pity, not softness, recognition.

"Yes," he said. "You do."

"Stop saying that. Stop, stop acting like you know me."

"I do know you." His voice was steady, heavy with something I didn't want to name. "I've always known you. Even before the night your mother died."

The clearing tightened around us.

"You don't get to say that," I whispered.

"You were nine," he said. "You hid in the cupboard. You heard her scream. You felt the shadows move through the walls. You begged someone to save you."

Every muscle in me locked.

"I came to you."

I shook my head hard, but the ground seemed to tilt, pulling me toward him.

"You fell asleep in my arms. And when you woke, they took it all away."

"No."

"I was yours. You were mine. Until they severed the thread."

He was so close I could see the faint pulse at the hollow of his throat, not human-quick, but slow, tidal.

"But you're remembering," he murmured. "Piece by piece. You feel it, don't you? In your spine. In your blood."

My hands were shaking. “Who are you?”

His smile was slow. Measured.

“You called me Taz. But my name is older than that. Older than your language. And it’s written across your skin whether you remember it or not.”

“This is a dream,” I said, forcing the words.

“Say that again.”

“This is a dream.”

He stepped forward. I stepped back. The trees behind me inhaled, their branches arching overhead, sealing the clearing in silver ribs.

“You can wake up,” he said. “But you’ll come back. You always do.”

“Why me?”

His eyes burned like a collapsing star.

“Because you are the key. Because you opened the door. Because I am yours, and you forgot.”

He raised his hand, not to touch me, but to show me.

In his palm, the spiral burned. Black, deep as a well.

The same one from my journal. From the patient logs. From the other dream.

"You're mad," I whispered.

His smile deepened.

"Well then," he said, "so are you."

Chapter Twelve

The Pattern

Róisín

I woke tangled in sweat-soaked sheets, heart battering my ribs like it was trying to break free, mouth dry enough to taste dust and copper.

The dream hadn't loosened its grip. It clung like wet fabric, heavy and stubborn, refusing to dissolve the way they usually did. The forest still lived behind my eyelids, the slow inhale of those pale, bone-ribbed trees, the silver shimmer along their trunks, the language threaded through their leaves. And him. Always him. His voice, honey lined with iron, curling around my ear like a promise I should never have heard. The spiral in his palm, black and bottomless, burned into memory as if my mind had pressed its face to it.

My thighs were still slick. My neck ached, not sharp pain but the lingering soreness of something having rested there too long. But it wasn't the physical aftermath that made me feel hollowed-out, it was the *knowing*. The way every detail had stayed sharp. Dreams weren't meant to survive daylight this clean.

I always forgot.

Not this time.

I sat up slowly, sheets peeling from my skin, and caught my reflection in the dark window, vague, washed in the orange smear of the streetlight. The glass turned it blurry, but my gut twisted anyway. I didn't trust the stillness. My eyes ached from holding its gaze, waiting for the smirk, the breath-fog bloom, the slow, delayed blink. Nothing came. Still, the muscle between my shoulder blades stayed clenched like a fist.

The air smelled faintly of smoke. Not candle smoke, sharper, older, the stale residue of something that had burned through to the end. I checked the sockets, the cords, the stove. Nothing. The smell stayed, curling through my lungs like it belonged there.

By the time I reached the lab, my skin was crawling under my hoodie. Sleeves pulled over my hands, head low, I tried to move like a shadow. But Jamie was waiting at my desk, posture casual in the way people make when they've been there too long.

"You didn't sleep again." It wasn't a question.

I didn't answer.

"You logged in at 2:43 a.m." His finger tapped the monitor beside my keyboard. "Not work-related. EEG archive access."

I stared at him. "How do you, "

"I have admin visibility," he cut in, too smooth. "You forgot to log out."

His tone was soft. Too soft. Not the warmth of a friend, but the coaxing calm you use on a stray you want close enough to catch.

"You okay?" he asked.

I nodded, but my neck felt like it was lying.

"You looked pale yesterday," he added, studying my face. "And you've been… different. Distant."

"I'm tired, Jamie."

"You've been tired for years."

That made me look at him properly. And I saw it. Not sympathy. Not even concern. Curiosity, the cold, surgical kind. The kind that doesn't want to help you, only own the understanding of you.

I stepped back from the desk. "Don't check my logs without asking."

"I was worried."

"You don't get to be."

I left before he could speak again.

⋆ ★ · ⋆ · ★ · ⋆ · ★

Siobhán caught me by the coffee machine, both hands wrapped around her mug like she meant to drink the heat before the tea.

"Hey, weird question," she said. "Were you here overnight?"

I frowned. "No."

"Strange. Motion sensor pinged on Level Two. You were the only name on the roster. Could've been a glitch, but…" She tilted her head. "It gave me déjà vu." She sipped. "Have you ever heard the name Mnemosyne?"

The syllables felt heavy before I even shaped them. "No," I said, too slowly. "What is it?"

"Found it scribbled on a clipboard outside Room C. Thought it was one of those biotech startups upstairs. Sounds Greek, right?"

I nodded, even as my pulse was crawling higher in my throat. "Maybe."

"Probably nothing. Nostalgia rebrand or whatever." She shrugged and left me there with the steam between us.

That afternoon, I went looking for Aisling's file. The girl who'd whispered, then screamed, my name.

It was gone.

No EEG. No intake. No discharge. Her profile scrubbed from the archive like she'd never walked through the doors.

Jamie said she'd been "transferred for further observation," but when I asked where, he shrugged. "Maybe psych?"

She wasn't psych. She'd been steady, even calm, until the dream swallowed her.

I dug deeper, backups, shadow archives, scratch folders where raw data lingers before the clean-up pass. Nothing. Not even a ghost file.

It was as though she'd been erased not just from the system, but from the building. From the face of the world.

That night, I pulled my mother's books from the back of the wardrobe, the ones I'd kept even when the covers disintegrated at the spine. Pressed leaves fell apart under my fingers. Margins crowded with her looping handwriting.

One thin volume stopped me. No title. Just a spiral stamped in faded black down the spine.

I opened it.

The first page was empty but for a single line, written in her hand:
Memory is the mother of dreams. Guard yours well, little one.

The word hooked itself under my ribs. *Memory.*

I turned the page and stopped. Written neatly in her ink, as though she'd meant me to find it years from now:

Mnemosyne

I sat on the floor with the book in my lap, my breath slow, shallow. Something is happening. I don't know yet if it's waking up or coming apart.

I told myself I wasn't going to look. That the scarf over the mirror would stay put. That I'd keep the rules I'd made for myself and get on with the day.

But rules thin out when you've been circling the same thought for hours, when the pressure behind your eyes feels like a knot you can't loosen.

Mid-afternoon, I found myself in the hallway, staring at the covered mirror. The scarf hung heavy, its knot slackened from too many quick ties. My fingers found the edge without my consent.

Just a peek. Daylight couldn't hurt.

I lifted the fabric an inch, then two.

The face staring back was mine, but the air behind her wasn't the hallway. It was dim, edges warped, colours bled to the blue-black of deep water. The skirting boards behind her rotted, wallpaper bubbling with damp. A shallow pool spread across the floor, catching a dull, sourceless light.

I leaned in. My reflection leaned too, but a fraction late. That delay made my stomach turn cold.

Somewhere beyond the glass, a faint knock. Not urgent. Not sharp. Just *there*.

I stepped back. The scarf slipped in my hand. I caught it and pulled it down hard, tying the knot twice, fingers clumsy.

My phone was already in my hand before I realised it. Fiadh's name glowed on the screen. Thumb hovering. I could almost hear her voice in my head, that clipped, cool tone she used when she didn't want to admit she was worried.

I ended the call before it rang.

Chapter Thirteen

Sleeptalkers & Warnings

Róisín

I made it three days without dreaming.

Three days of forcing my body into knots, muscles held tight enough that my jaw clicked when I chewed, blinking through caffeine burn, willing myself to exist in that dull, brittle space where sleep can't quite get its claws in. If I stayed awake long enough, if I kept moving, nothing could reach me.

It didn't work.

Even without the dreams, the air felt thinner now, like I'd been dropped into a room that wasn't airtight, someone else's lungs syncing their rise and fall with mine. I could almost feel the pause before each exhale, as though they were waiting to hear if I'd breathe next.

The hallway lights stuttered when I swiped into the lab. Again. The hum in the wiring was louder than it should have been, not an audible buzz exactly, but a vibration in my teeth.

Siobhán looked up from the breakroom as I passed. "You look like you've seen a ghost," she said, half-joking, but her eyes didn't match her tone.

I tried to smile. It didn't stick.

Jamie was already at my desk. He's always at my desk now. I don't know if it's conscious or instinct, but he hovers like a shadow that's learned speech.

"You didn't sleep again," he said, not a question.

I dropped my bag and logged in without looking at him.

His voice softened into that careful register people use when they want you to give them something. "I checked your activity. You were in the EEG archives again. Two in the morning."

"You're watching my log-ins now?"

"You left your account open," he said, like that excused it. "I'm just… concerned."

"No, Jamie." I met his eyes. "You're fucking nosey."

That shut him up, but only for a beat.

"You've been… different lately," he said finally. "It's not just tired. It's something else."

"If you think I'm seeing things, just say it."

His mouth pressed into a line. "Are you?"

I didn't answer. Because I didn't want to give him the satisfaction, and because I wasn't entirely sure anymore.

★ ★ ★ ★ ★ ★ ★

Before lunch, one of the interns, Emma, flagged me down outside Room B.

"Subject 056," she said. "You should hear this."

She pulled up the EEG feed and slid me a headset.

The pattern hit me first. Not the spikes, the rhythm. Those tight, repeating curves, symmetrical but wrong. I'd seen them before. In my own data from the night of the forest dream.

Identical.

Emma scrubbed back the playback. The patient's breathing was slow, deep, the rustle of sheets soft in the background. Then, the whisper.

"Taz… come back…"

My stomach went cold.

Emma frowned. “What’s a Taz?”

I handed the headset back carefully, like I was holding something fragile I didn’t want to break, or acknowledge. “No idea. Lock this file. Restricted review only.”

She blinked. “Uh. Okay?”

★ ★ · ★ · ★ · ★ · ★

I stepped outside, into air that at least pretended to be fresh, even if it still tasted faintly of rain and bus fumes.

My phone buzzed in my pocket. Voicemail.

Fiadh’s voice, sharp-edged, almost breaking:

“Róisín… it’s about Dad. Something he still has, mom left it with him. You need to be careful. Just… call me, okay?”

The message ended mid-breath. No explanation. No follow-up.

Back home, the flat felt wrong in the way it sometimes does, like someone’s been there, but only long enough to leave the air rearranged.

I pulled my mother’s book from under the bed, the one with the spiral burned down the spine. I’d avoided it for years, ever since I found it in the bottom of a box after her funeral, the leather brittle, the edges water-warped.

I flipped past the first page.

Her handwriting filled the next, cramped but precise, the way she always wrote when she thought something mattered:

The thread binds the dreamer to what waits beyond the wall. Sever it, and you sever the self. Memory is the anchor. Memory is the key.

The further I read, the tighter my chest felt.

The door opens both ways. The wrong hand will turn it.

The mark calls the one who shaped it.

A page later: a small ink drawing of the spiral, mine now, though I'd never known it was hers first.

I shut the book. Sat there in the dark, listening for nothing, hearing too much.

And then,

Low. Close. Right beside my ear.

"Little Star."

Not in the dream. Not in that float-state between awake and asleep.

Awake.

And he was here.

The air shifted, warm against the side of my neck, carrying the faint scent of cedar and something metallic. My skin prickled all the way to my fingertips.

Somewhere in the hallway, the scarf over the mirror shifted, a faint, deliberate rustle, like breath pushing against fabric.

I didn't move.

Because some part of me, the part that remembered the weight of his hand in the forest, the slow lean of him in the mirror room, was terrified that if I turned my head, I wouldn't find empty space.

I'd find him.

And worse, I'd let him stay.

Chapter Fourteen

The Drowning Room

Róisín

I didn't drift off. I slipped under.

One moment, I was sitting cross-legged in the dark with my mother's book balanced on my knees, the spiral stamped on its spine pressed into my palm like it could brand me if I held it long enough. My heartbeat was unsteady, palms clammy against the worn leather.

Then next, I was here.

Standing.

Barefoot. Naked.

The room around me breathed.

The ceiling arched impossibly high, a ballroom half-swallowed by shadow. Chandeliers swayed overhead, their crystals scattering fractured light over walls mottled with damp, as though the building had been left to rot for centuries and only just remembered how to hold itself upright.

The air smelled of cold stone and old smoke, the same smoke that had followed me from my flat to the lab bathroom mirror, to the fogged glass of the shower. It wasn't a scent you forgot.

Water lapped at my ankles. Icy. It wrapped around my skin like something with fingers. I could hear it seeping in through unseen cracks, a slow, patient trickle that didn't match how quickly it was rising.

"This isn't real," I whispered.

The water climbed to my calves. The cold wasn't passive, it threaded itself through my muscles, settling in my bones.

I turned, searching for a wall, a door, anything solid to anchor to. The room shifted instead. The corners slid away from me. The space tightened.

The doors were gone.

"Stop," I whispered to the empty air. "Please stop."

A sound answered, silk dragged over bare skin.

"Little Star."

I spun. Breath locked sharp in my throat.

He stood waist-deep in the water, watching me. His bare chest caught what little light the chandeliers spilled. Hair damp and curling against his temples. And those eyes, galaxies folding inward, gravity made visible, the same impossible burn I'd seen at the lab sink.

My knees weakened.

"You're not real," I forced out, my voice splintering.

He moved toward me through the water. Slow. Certain. The surface barely rippled around him, as if it obeyed him.

"You say that every time."

"Because it's true."

His mouth curved, not amusement. Indulgence. The way you humour a child who's wrong.

"Is it?"

The water reached my stomach. My skin was shaking under the cold.

"You're a hallucination," I whispered. "Sleep deprivation. My brain is failing."

"You've been failing for years," he said softly, almost kindly. "And yet… here I am. Every time you close your eyes, you find me."

The water surged higher. It swirled against my ribs, pulling me toward him. My toes lost the floor. I went under.

Cold roared in my ears. It flooded my nose. Filled my mouth.

I kicked hard, lungs burning, until his hands closed around my waist and I was hauled up like I weighed nothing.

I broke the surface coughing, choking on air. His arms locked around me. My breasts pressed to his chest. My thighs wrapped instinctively around his hips, the only way to keep above the water. The hard line of his cock pushed against me through the swirl of current.

"Let me go," I said, though my voice was thin and trembling, my body already betraying me.

"You don't want that."

The way he said it, low, absolute, cracked something in me. His lips brushed my ear. Not quite a kiss.

"You came back to me."

The water kept climbing. It licked at my collarbones, tugged my hair, wrapped the cold around me like rope. I clung harder, grinding helplessly against the heat of him, just to remind myself there was warmth somewhere in this place.

"This isn't real," I tried again, but the slow, involuntary roll of my hips made the words hollow.

His teeth grazed my jaw.

"Say that while you're dripping for me."

The words hit something old. My clit pulsed with every grind against him, raw heat blooming under the cold.

"You used to beg for me in your sleep, Little Star," he murmured, one hand gripping my thigh tighter, spreading me wider in the water. The movement made me sink just enough for the cold to close over my shoulders. My nipples peaked instantly, aching under the bite of it, then warmed again against his chest.

I moaned. My thighs trembled against him.

"You can pretend you don't remember," he said, "but your body never forgot."

His hand slid lower, finding my clit under the water. The first stroke was slow enough to hurt. The second had my head falling back, chandeliers swinging above like pendulums counting down the seconds until I broke.

The water climbed higher. Over my chin. I tilted my head back, gasping against the flood.

"You can fight me," he murmured, his thumb circling harder, "but you won't."

The water kissed my mouth. My lips parted around a gasp I couldn't catch. His hand clamped harder on my thigh, grinding me against him until my clit throbbed in rhythm with my pulse.

And then, molten, unyielding.

"My Goddess".

The sound ignited something deep and buried.

A shard of memory rose, me, smaller, curled in his lap in the dark, his voice saying the same words as if they belonged to me.

I came hard, choking on the scream as water surged over my head. The orgasm rolled through me in waves, every muscle locking as I clung to him under the surface, the cold and heat colliding until I couldn't tell them apart.

He kept me under a beat too long. My chest burned. When his grip loosened, I reached for him instead of the surface.

I hated myself for it, even as I breathed him in.

Everything dissolved.

I woke gasping in my flat. Sweat slicked my skin. My thighs trembled. My pussy still pulsed like I hadn't left him at all.

The mirror was still covered. The flat was silent.

But my body knew better.

And the worst part? I was already waiting for the water to take me again.

I sat by the window with the lights off, watching Galway Bay shift under the moon. The tide was coming in slow, patient, licking the seawall like it was tasting the stone.

My tea had gone cold in my hands. Somewhere out there, past the black line of the horizon, he was waiting.

I could almost feel the pull of it. Steady as the tide. And just as impossible to stop.

Chapter Fifteen

Undertow

Taz

She thinks the Drowning Room was an accident. A glitch in the machinery of her exhausted mind. A fever hallucination conjured by sleeplessness and stress.

She doesn't understand.

I built it for her.

Every dream she's had, and every dream she's been denied, has been a piece of the map. I've been drawing it for years. Patient and surgical. A cartographer of her mind. I have spent nights standing in the dark behind her, my shadow brushing the curve of her back, adjusting horizons by degrees. Tilting corridors a fraction to the left. Stitching symbols into corners like threads only she could follow. I've carved landmarks into her subconscious with the care of an architect building for a queen.

You don't drag someone this deep all at once. You let them wander first. You let them believe each step is theirs.

There were places she never reached, but they're still waiting.

A garden overgrown with black roses that bleed when touched, petals bruised with moonlight. A library where every book melts into water the second she turns a page, the words dissolving into ripples that lap at her wrists. A stairwell that winds downward forever, unless she turns around and looks at me, and only then does it end.

Some nights she would come close enough to smell the sea behind the walls. She'd pause, head tilted, pulse stumbling, instinct telling her that one step further would change everything. And then she'd wake, shaking her head at nothing, and the door would vanish again.

Other nights she walked straight into the snares I'd set. Hallways lined with mirrors that breathed back at her. Train stations with no trains, the speaker whispering her name instead of destinations. A chapel whose altar was already laid out for her arrival, candles flickering in a draft that existed only in dreams.

Every one of them a test. Every one of them teaching her body to remember me, even when her mind refused.

And then, finally, she stepped into the Drowning Room.

The chandeliers, the slick stone, the cold water that never stopped rising, none of it was chance. It was the final chamber in a route I'd been carving through her since we were children. I'd been patient enough to let her forget me, just so I could watch her remember.

I felt the shock ripple through her when the first lick of cold touched her ankles. The water climbed in slow, deliberate increments, calves, knees, seeping into her bones. Her pulse quickened, that little tremor in her breathing betraying her. Her mind scrambled for an explanation, but water doesn't care about explanations. It climbs regardless.

She tried to back away. The walls shifted because I wanted them to. She pleaded, small and human, and the water rose faster.

When it closed over her ribs, she was mine.

She slipped under, and I let her. I let the weight press into her chest, let her lungs seize, let her taste that sharp, aching terror that forces surrender. I kept her there long enough for her to feel herself coming apart, then I took her back.

The moment my hands closed on her waist, her body remembered me. It wasn't thought. It wasn't choice. It was recognition. Her thighs locked around my hips like she'd done it a thousand times, like the years between us had never been carved away.

Her skin was slick and cold under my palms, but inside she was molten. The first grind of her pussy over my cock wasn't deliberate, it was instinct, muscle memory, a reflex older than her fear.

And I savoured it. Gods, I have waited years to feel that again.

She whispered that I wasn't real even as she moved against me, desperate for friction. I let her keep the lie, because lies make the truth sharper when they finally cut.

Her clit throbbed under my thumb, the beat matching my own pulse. Every shiver of her hips, every gasp torn from her throat, I stored away like scripture. I felt her tighten around the absence inside her, her body screaming yes while her mouth still mouthed no.

And then I told her she was my Goddess.

Not because I needed her to hear it, but because I needed her to *feel* it. To let those words sink into her marrow, anchoring themselves in places she doesn't even admit exist. I've been patient. I've been careful. But that night, I wanted to see her break in my hands again.

She shattered for me.

Her muscles locked. Her voice broke against my ear. The chandeliers swung overhead like pendulums. The water churned and the walls shook, as though the whole room recognised what was happening. The thread between us, the real one, the one no one can sever, pulled tight enough that I could feel it hum.

I could have let her wake gently. I didn't.

I let her surface in her own bed gasping, lungs burning, her pussy still clenching around the ghost of me. So she'd know it wasn't just a dream. So, she'd lie there in the dark with her thighs still trembling and realise I was *still with her*.

The map is almost complete now. She's walked the breathing forest. Stood in the mirror room. Drowned in the ballroom.

She's touched my traps without recognising them. There are only a few doors left.

And when the last one opens, I won't need her to close her eyes. I'll pull her under while she's awake, and she will thank me for it.

Chapter Sixteen

Static & Seduction
Róisín

The air felt too thin. Even in daylight. Even in the sterile hum of the lab.

Except… the hum wasn't sterile anymore. It wasn't background. It had weight, a density that pressed on the sides of my head until it felt like it was inside my skull. The vibrations seemed to carry something in them, a pulse threaded through the electricity, like the walls were holding their breath for me.

The lights flickered as I walked the hallway, that quick stutter of illumination everyone else chalked up to faulty wiring. For me, it was the blink of an eye. A twitch in reality. And in that half-second of dim, I thought I saw him.

Not fully. Not the clean outline of a man. Just a distortion in the corner of my vision, as if a shadow had been stretched too long and warped across the glass of the observation room. A shimmer like heat above tarmac, the faintest suggestion of movement where there should have been none.

I blinked.

Gone.

My fingers trembled against the badge scanner. The light on the reader pulsed once, twice, before giving the grudging click that unlocked the door. It didn't feel like a mechanical delay. It felt like something on the other side was considering me before deciding to let me through.

The morning slid past in broken frames. I kept my eyes on the monitor, forcing myself to read the lines of EEG data, but the numbers swam. They wouldn't resolve into meaning. My mind kept circling back to the irregularities. Sharp bursts. Jagged spirals blooming in patients with no sleep anomalies in their history. Identical patterns appearing across cases that had nothing in common.

It wasn't just here. It wasn't just the lab.

On the way in that morning, I'd stopped at the corner shop for a bottle of water. The place was nearly empty, the only sound the low mechanical hum of the fridge units. I stood by the counter, letting my eyes wander to the wall of warped mirrors behind the cigarette display. They were cheap, the kind designed to keep customers aware they were being watched, but one of them…

One of them fogged over. Just for a second. As though someone had pressed their mouth against it from the inside.

I stepped closer before I even thought about it, the cold bottle sweating in my palm. My reflection stared back, tired eyes, hair pulled into a knot, but in the blur of the glass there was something else. A faint, dark outline standing just behind my shoulder. Taller. Still. Waiting.

I blinked, and the fog was gone. The space behind me empty.

The cashier cleared his throat, and I realised he'd been watching me stare at nothing. I paid, mumbled thanks, and left without looking at him again.

* * *

I kept walking, I passed the laundrette. One of the wall-mounted CCTV monitors flickered just as I came into view. It should have been showing the inside of the shop, the neat rows of humming dryers, the lone man folding shirts at the back, but the image stuttered, and the picture froze.

On the frozen feed was me. Standing exactly where I was now. Except in the CCTV reflection, there was someone else. Behind me. Too close.

The frame blinked again, and the feed was back to normal. The man inside the laundrette was still folding his shirts, blissfully unaware.

I didn't look into any more windows after that.

The spiral kept finding me.

In the margins of printouts from other people's stations. In the corner of calibration notes I didn't remember writing. In my personal notebook, pages deep, where my handwriting looped into it over and over without me realising.

It was no longer just a shape. It felt like a fracture. A hairline crack running across the inside of my mind.

* * * * * * *

And Jamie was there again. Always close. Always *too* close.

"You didn't answer my texts last night," he said. His tone was light, but his stance was calculated, hip against the edge of my desk, head angled down so his voice dropped low enough for no one else to hear.

"I was sleeping," I lied.

"That's good. You need rest."

His eyes skimmed over me in a way that made my skin crawl, not leering, but cataloguing. Assessing. Like he wanted to see where the edges were weakest.

"I'm fine," I said.

"You keep saying that."

Then his voice shifted, softened in that deliberate way people use when they want to sound like the only safe place left in the room. "You know… sometimes when people are going through things, they need someone who understands. You don't have to keep pushing me away."

It made my stomach knot. The way he said *understands*. Like it was both an offer and a possession.

"You don't understand," I said, sharper than I meant to.

He flinched, a flicker, quickly masked by a faint smile. "You're right. But I want to."

The weight of that *want* sat between us like an object I couldn't step around.

I stood abruptly. "I need to check the calibration logs."

He moved, but only far enough for me to pass.

The equipment room was dim, the hum of the machines thick in the air. I shut the door behind me and let the darkness press against my skin. Pressed my palms into my thighs. Tried to steady my breath.

My phone buzzed.

When I pulled it out, the screen shimmered, a ripple of static crawling across it, not the glitch of bad reception but the texture of interference, as if something was *inside* the signal. The Wi-Fi was perfect. Full bars.

The static cleared and there it was.

A text. No number. No name. Just one line:

I can feel you breaking for me.

The words landed like a hand closing around my chest. My stomach dropped. My mouth went dry.

The hum in the room deepened. It wasn't machine noise anymore. It had warmth. Presence.

The scent hit next, cedar, smoke, rain on stone, not faint, not imagined, but here, in the air I was breathing.

The shadows at the far wall shifted.

"You're not here," I whispered. "You can't be here."

The monitors flared black, static rushing through their screens in unison before clearing again. The distortion moved through the wires like it was alive, threading through the room with purpose.

Heat brushed the back of my neck. My nipples tightened so sharply under my blouse that I bit down on a sound. My thighs pressed together without thought.

I didn't turn.

Fingers, not quite touching, but close enough to feel, traced down the line of my arm, an almost-contact that made my breath stumble.

"Stop," I rasped, though it came out weak.

No answer.

My pulse had migrated south, throbbing between my legs, each beat a demand. My body remembered him too well. The water. The weight. The ache that came after.

"You're not here," I tried again, but this time it was almost a plea.

The voice slid into my ear, velvet over steel.

"You're already mine, Little Star."

The heat of it rolled through me, making my knees want to fold. My hand twitched downward, a traitor move toward the ache, before my mind caught up.

Not here. Not now.

I forced my eyes open. The warmth withdrew. The machines resumed their ordinary hum. But my reflection in the dead-black screen opposite me didn't feel ordinary.

I watched it. Waited for it to smirk.

It didn't.

Still, I didn't trust it.

* * . * . * . * *

Later, at home, I sat cross-legged on the floor in front of my covered mirror. The scarf hung heavy over it, the knot pulled tight. My breath was still unsteady. My palms still itched from the ghost of his touch.

I hated myself for it. For the way my body leaned forward, just slightly, like it wanted me to pull the fabric away. For the truth that curled low in my gut.

I wanted him.

And I wasn't sure I'd fight next time.

Chapter Seventeen

The Silent Cathedral

Róisín & Taz

Roisin

I knew where I was the moment the air thickened. It clung to me like wet velvet, heavy and close, every breath tasting faintly of stone and something older, salt? Blood? The memory of smoke curling from an extinguished altar.

The cathedral rose around me in silence, its pale columns arching like the ribs of something that had once been alive and impossibly large. Above, the black dome stretched so high it seemed to pull gravity toward it, swallowing the light. And there was light, fractured beams bleeding from stained glass panels whose colors didn't belong to any spectrum I knew. The patterns shifted if I looked too long: flowers blooming into eyes, spirals curling into open mouths. They painted the damp floor in trembling, liquid hues that rippled as though the stone were breathing with me.

I was naked again. I always was now. I had stopped asking why.

The silence wasn't empty. It was *waiting*. Every surface felt poised, as if the entire building held its breath for what came next.

And then he was there. Emerging from shadow the way smoke curls from a hidden flame, soundless, inevitable, and absolutely certain of himself.

My stomach clenched. My pulse stumbled into an unsteady, too-loud rhythm that filled my ears. His gaze caught me instantly. Those eyes, violet and blue galaxies spinning slow and deep, pulling me toward them even as every survival instinct screamed *stay still*.

"Not again," I whispered, though my voice betrayed me with the tremor I couldn't control.

"You came," he said. Not as an accusation, not as a question, simply stating what was true.

"No." I shook my head, but the word felt hollow. "I don't want this."

"You do."

The words slid over my skin like heat poured from a cup, sinking into muscle and bone. My nipples tightened under the weight of them. My thighs pressed together without thought, chasing a friction that wasn't there.

"You're in my head," I said, trying to steady my breath. "You're not real."

His mouth curved, slow and deliberate. "Your mother made sure of that."

The words hit low, cutting through my ribs. "My… mother?"

"She made the bargain," he said, voice rich with something between reverence and scorn. "Tore us apart. Severed your thread. But even that couldn't keep you from finding me again."

I stumbled back, bare feet silent against the cold floor, even as the light seemed to follow me. "I don't remember."

"You weren't supposed to."

He moved toward me with the slow certainty of a man who knew how the story ended. Every step seemed to lengthen the shadows behind him, stretching them along the ribs of the cathedral until they loomed over us like guardians.

"She begged Mnemosyne to take your dreams. To lock your memories away. To *protect* you from me."

The way he said protect made the word sound like blasphemy.

"She thought she could keep you safe," he murmured, almost tenderly. "But you were mine first."

The cathedral's fractured light crawled over his bare chest, painting him in shards of sacred and profane.

"You don't remember what you were meant to be," he said softly, "but your body does."

His hand lifted, fingertips grazing the underside of my jaw. My breath caught hard in my throat, my whole body leaning toward the touch like it had been waiting for years.

"You should have been mine," he whispered. "The first. The only."

And the ache in his voice made something deep in me twist like it had been hooked.

Taz

The moment my fingers touched her jaw, I felt it, that hum under her skin, electric and alive, the one that had haunted me through every empty century without her.

I'd mapped this moment in the dark a thousand times. Every dream she didn't have, I still did. I walked these halls alone in her absence, picturing her here: her bare feet on the damp floor, her breath catching when my thumb brushed her lip. I had taught myself patience because I had to. But patience is not the same as mercy.

My touch drifted, tracing the curve of her neck, the delicate notch of her collarbone. I felt her pulse stutter against my fingers. She was trying to hold herself upright, trying to pretend her knees weren't already soft.

She has been touched by others. I can smell it, faint traces clinging like dust in the corners of her skin. I will burn it out of her. I will unmake every ghost of them until there is no part of her that doesn't remember I was here first.

My palm flattened against her stomach. Her inhale was sharp, a shiver rippling through her muscles. I didn't move lower yet. Let her ache. Let her feel the absence as much as the promise.

The cathedral seemed to lean closer. Columns groaned quietly, stained glass pulsing like the walls themselves remembered her too.

I lowered my mouth to her ear, close enough for my breath to stir the fine hairs at her neck. "You don't remember," I murmured, "but your body has never stopped calling for me."

Her exhale was shaky. Beautiful. Good. This is only the beginning.

Róisín

His hand on my stomach was the only thing tethering me to the floor. He didn't grip. Didn't push lower. Just rested there, warm and impossibly steady, like a weight I'd been carrying my whole life without knowing it.

The heat of him seeped into me until I swayed toward him, thighs pressing together, the ache between them tightening into something sharp. My breathing came shallow, uneven. His scent wrapped around me, cedar, smoke, rain on hot stone, until I wanted to inhale nothing else.

"You don't remember," he said again, voice slipping under my skin, "but your body has never stopped calling for me."

Something clenched low in my belly. My nipples were so tight they ached in the cool air.

Then his hand moved, sliding lower, tracing the hard line of my hipbone, curling his fingers toward the inside of my thigh. My knees softened, traitorous. I leaned in, just enough for his fingers to find me.

The walls of the cathedral began to hum, the sound so low it was more vibration than noise. Light spilled over him in fractured waves, as if even the building wanted to touch him.

When his palm brushed the heat between my thighs, I gasped. He didn't cup me. Not yet. His fingertips traced the inner line of my leg, feather-light, until my body trembled from the wanting.

His chest touched my back now, barely, but the contact lit every nerve in my spine. There was no space between us anymore that felt right.

“I should have been your first,” he whispered into my ear, voice like smoke curling into my lungs.

The words pierced something I didn’t know was still intact.

His other hand tilted my head so my neck arched, mouth hovering just above my skin. I could feel the heat of his lips without the kiss, and it was maddening.

When his fingers finally slid up between my folds, I choked on a gasp. My hips bucked forward, seeking more, and he gave it in increments, slow, deliberate circles over my clit, dragging the pleasure out until my legs shook.

“You don’t belong untouched,” he murmured. “And I won’t let you be.”

The cathedral seemed to sway. My hands grabbed for a column, its cold surface grounding me while he worked me apart with nothing but his hand and his voice.

“That’s it… give me everything.”

A moan broke loose before I could stop it. His grip on my jaw tightened, keeping my head where he wanted it, as two fingers slid into me, curling into the spot that made my vision blur.

Somewhere above us, the stained glass cracked, a slow spiderweb of light spilling down like a blessing or a curse.

He thrust deeper. My hips met his, frantic now, desperate for the release hovering just out of reach.

"Cum for me, Little Star."

I broke. My body clamped around his fingers, pleasure crashing through me so hard I cried out against the cold stone, my knees shaking. His arm wrapped tight around my waist, holding me until I'd ridden the last shuddering wave.

Then, low and certain against my ear:

"I love it when you break for me."

The cathedral went silent again. When I opened my eyes, he was gone.

Chapter Eighteen

His Hunger

Taz

She is so close to breaking I can taste it. It's in the way her breath catches when she sees me, not just in the dream, but in the slick reflection of shop windows, in the black glass of a monitor screen, in the corner of her waking vision where she dares herself not to look twice. It's in the way her thighs press together when I close the distance between us, the way her body braces as if she knows the air will feel heavier with me in it.

She still whispers denials like spells, *you're not real, you're not here*, as if words have the power to unmake me. She still pretends her unraveling is incidental, some side effect of exhaustion. But I know the truth.

Her body knows me. Remembers me. And her body has never lied.

I have been building this road to her for years. The Mirror Room to make her feel my eyes. The Forest to give her back fragments of what they took. The Drowning Room to force her to reach for me when there was nothing else to hold. The Cathedral… to bring her to her knees.

She thinks the dreams are random, but they are constellations, each placed and connected, a map stitched into the dark.

I should have been her first, her only, and I would have been, if they hadn't severed the thread.

Her mother went to Mnemosyne herself, on her knees in the dream-realm, begging her to take my face from Róisín's mind. To erase my voice from her memory. To lock away every night we'd shared. She wanted her daughter to grow without me, to believe she'd been untouched.

But the truth is this: we had already bound ourselves. We had stood together in the observatory. We had been nine years old. And even then, she was mine.

I remember it in every detail. The observatory wasn't steel and glass the way mortals build them. It was grown from bone-white arches that curved into a perfect dome of midnight. The air was warm and thin, smelling faintly of salt and iron. The floor beneath our bare feet was smooth as still water, though it rang faintly when we moved, like some great instrument hidden under the stone.

The stars weren't pinned to the sky. They hung loose, drifting, some no bigger than a candle flame, others the size of our hands. Each one gave off a soft hum that you felt in your teeth before you heard it.

She stood beside me in her nightdress, the hem brushing her knees, her hair wild from sleep and smelling faintly of the sea. Her toes curled against the floor as if she knew she stood somewhere that wasn't meant for ordinary feet.

"Where do they go?" she asked, holding a pale-gold star between her hands. It pulsed faintly, speaking to her in a language she didn't yet understand.

"Where you put them," I told her.

I opened my palms, and the glow in her hands brightened, not from the star, but from me. The old light in my blood flowed through my skin into hers, weaving a current between us. Her lips parted, and I saw the reflection of the dome's starlight trembling in her eyes.

She laughed then. It was not the guarded, brittle thing I hear from her now, but bright and alive, the sound of a child who had not yet been taught to hide her joy. The whole dome answered her, the starlight rippling like water disturbed by a thrown stone.

We placed the stars together, one in the east, one in the north, moving in patterns older than we were, older than the world. Threads of light pulled taut between them until constellations bloomed above.

By the end, her palms glowed faintly too. She looked down at them, frowning as if they belonged to someone else.

"You're part of this," I told her. "Part of me."

She tilted her head, unsure, but nodded slowly, the way you do when you don't understand yet but can feel the truth settling in your bones.

That was the night they began to fear what we were becoming.
That was the night her mother decided to cut the thread.

The memory frays there, splintering into light. I know what came after, but she doesn't. Not yet.

And memory is not death. It is a tide. And tides always return.

Now, she comes to me naked in her sleep, exposed before I even lay a hand on her. And when I do, when my fingers slide between her thighs and find the heat that's been waiting for me all these years, she trembles. She melts. She grinds her clit against my palm like her body has been holding its breath for me.

Her pussy tells me everything her mouth won't. Slick. Open. Hungry.

She hates it. She needs it. That exquisite war between denial and craving is the most beautiful thing I have ever seen.

I could take her in the Cathedral now, spread her across the altar, bind her wrists above her head, sink into her until the columns groaned and the stained glass shattered from the sound of her screaming my name.

Not gentle. Not soft. The way gods take what belongs to them.

I imagine her voice breaking, begging as I push her through climax after climax until she forgets where she ends and I begin.

"Please, Taz… please, I can't, "

"Yes, you can, Little Star. You will. For me."

Her mother thought she could bury this, that years and silence would starve it out.

But I have been patient. I have let my hunger sharpen into something holy.

Now, even when she wakes, she feels me, between her thighs, in the static at the edge of her thoughts, in the air that thickens when she's alone.

She is waking. And soon, she will beg to be broken.

I will make her beg. And when she does, I will not stop. Not until she is mine again. Completely.

Chapter Nineteen

The Watcher's Confession
Róisín & Taz

Roisin

The knock came just after midnight.

Not polite. Not neighbourly. The kind of knock that made the frame shudder and sent a ripple through the glass like it wanted to shiver itself out of place.

I was sitting on the floor with my back to the bed, the spiral-covered book heavy across my thighs. The duvet was still twisted from the last time I'd tried to sleep. I hadn't changed the sheets since the cathedral dream, they still smelled faintly of him, like cedar smoke clinging to stone. My skin still remembered him in ways I didn't want to name.

The knock came again. Louder.

When I opened the door, Fiadh stood there, hair damp from the mist outside, strands clinging to her cheek. She looked… wrong. Too pale, eyes too wide, chest heaving like she'd run the whole way across Galway and hadn't decided if she should stop yet.

"Jesus, Fiadh, "

"I couldn't wait anymore." Her voice was tight, clipped, but under it was a strange vibration, not just fear, but urgency honed sharp enough to cut.

She pushed past me without asking, scanning the flat like she expected someone else to be inside. Her gaze snagged on the covered mirror and stayed there. Not just looking, staring, like it was a stranger in the room that might start speaking at any moment.

When she finally looked back at me, her eyes dropped to the book in my hands. Her expression shifted in a way that made my stomach dip.

"You've been dreaming again." Not a question.

I frowned. "What?"

"You were never supposed to wake."

The words didn't land so much as hover in the air between us, heavy enough that my brain refused to pick them up. I just stood there, waiting for them to make sense. They didn't.

"Fiadh, "

"You need to know before it's too late."

Her pacing started then, sharp turns across my small living room, hands flexing at her sides like she didn't know what to do with them. A strand of hair slipped free from its tie and she pushed it back without noticing, her focus fixed somewhere else entirely.

"Mom wasn't what you thought."

"She was my mother," I said, each word slow.

"She was more than that," Fiadh said, her voice climbing over mine like she couldn't risk letting me interrupt. "She carried blood older than this world. She was one of Urania's children, "

I held up a hand. "The what?"

"Urania," she pressed on, almost breathless now, "daughter of Mnemosyne, "

"Fiadh, you sound like you're reading me a Wikipedia page after a bottle of wine."

"She was a muse. Muse of memory and stars. That blood passed to mom. And mom passed it to you."

The air felt heavier again, not because I believed her, but because she believed her, and belief changes the shape of a room.

"You realise how mad this sounds?" I said.

“She tried to hide it. To protect you from him.”

“The him who’s currently… what? Haunting my REM cycles?” I laughed, sharp and joyless, trying to slice the tension in half.

Her jaw tightened. “From Taz.”

The name hit like a cold hand between my shoulder blades.

“He isn’t Titan-born. He’s Phantasos. One of the Oneiroi. A god of dreams.”

“Oh, of course. Sure.” I gestured vaguely upward. “God of dreams. That’ll look great in the lab’s incident report.”

“He rules in images. In water. In mirrors,” she said, voice hardening. “He can make you forget what’s real. And he’s drawn to our bloodline, always has been.”

“Why?” I asked, because part of me wanted to hear how far she’d take it.

“Because you carry constellations in your blood. Because the thread between you was dangerous.”

I barked a laugh that didn’t sound like mine. “So, I’ve been cosmically pen-palling a dream god since childhood?”

“Yes,” she said without hesitation. “And you gave him something before you even knew what it was worth.”

A strange pressure gathered behind my eyes, flashes of something I couldn't quite hold black sky, my hands glowing faintly, laughter that made my ribs ache. I shoved it away.

"Mom saw it," she said. "She begged Mnemosyne to cut the thread. To bury your dreams. To take your memories before you were lost completely."

I couldn't answer. Not because I didn't have words, but because my mouth wouldn't open.

Her gaze slid back to the mirror. "Once the thread is rewoven, it can't be cut again."

"Fiadh," I said slowly, "I don't know what's going on with you, but this? This isn't helping. If you think I'm in trouble, maybe call literally anyone who isn't… you, right now."

Her mouth flattened into something that wasn't quite a smile. "You think the danger is only him. It's not. There are others. And they won't care if you burn."

She left without waiting for me to throw her out. The door clicked shut behind her, sharp, final, like a period at the end of a sentence I couldn't read.

I stood there for a long time, staring at the scarf over the mirror, my skin prickling. I didn't want to think about the way her voice had cracked on the word burn.

⋆ ★ · ⋆ · ★ · ⋆ ˙ ★

Taz

Her sister's truths are crooked things, half-light, half-shadow, but even half a truth cuts deeper than a lie.

I have walked her dreams longer than she's had a name for herself. Even when they cut the thread, I felt her, faint as starlight through fog, but there. Always there.

She doesn't remember the first night. I do.

We were both nine. She didn't know my name, didn't know what I was, but she carried a jar in her hands, no bigger than a heart. Inside it: light. Not candlelight, not fire, something older, the exact shade of the stars that marked her bloodline. She had made it herself.

She offered it to me.

And with it, she offered herself. Not in the mortal way, not flesh, not vows, but in the old language of dreams, where a gift given freely binds tighter than chains.

The moment I touched it, the thread wove itself between us.

That night we built a sky together. The observatory was bone-white and ribbed in arches, the dome above alive with slow-moving stars. They hummed softly, each one warm to the touch. She laughed when I set one in place, the sound unguarded, so bright the dome echoed it back like it wanted to keep it.

She traced a spiral into my palm without knowing it spelled my name. I told her she was part of this, part of me. She didn't understand, but she nodded like she could feel it anyway.

Then they came for her.

I remember the storm in her waking world, the slam of a cupboard door, the crash of something breaking. I remember the mirror fracturing like ice as hands reached through to drag her away. Her mother's voice, sharp with fear. Her own voice, screaming mine until the sound tore from her throat.

Mnemosyne herself severed the thread. Burned my name from her dreams. Left me to walk empty rooms, my footsteps the only sound. Do you know what it is to touch every wall, memorise every corner, knowing exactly who is missing? It is a hunger that doesn't die.

Years passed. Mortals forgot. I didn't.

And now, the thread hums again. She wakes with my name in her mouth, her thighs damp from dreams she won't speak aloud. Her body remembers what they stole.

This is not discovery. This is reclamation.

She will fight. She will call me sickness. But in the dream, she is mine, and when the last of her denial burns away, she will remember the jar of starlight, the sky we built, and the truth her sister only half-knows.

And when she remembers, I will take her completely.

Chapter Twenty

The Dream Feast
Róisín & Taz

Róisín

The dream did not begin.

It swallowed me.

One breath I was in my flat, knees drawn to my chest, the spiral-covered book clutched so tight my knuckles ached. The next, the world tipped and I was standing barefoot in the centre of a vast, black hall.

The air here had weight. Metallic on my tongue, faintly sweet like old stone after rain. Every noise arrived softened, as if I were hearing from the bottom of a pool. Under my soles, the marble pulsed in slow intervals, warm under one foot, cool under the other, as if the floor was a living thing taking tidal breaths.

A table ran the length of the hall, too long for human use, disappearing into distances that could not exist indoors. It was set for a feast and everything on it was wrong. Almost real, but slant, like copies of earthly things made by something that had only been told about them. A roast bird gleamed with oil-slick colours that did not belong in any kitchen. Bowls of fruit wore shadows that bled into the cloth in bruised stains. Crystal goblets brimmed with a liquid that shifted each time I blinked, wine then ink then something thicker that clung to the glass in slow sheets.

Candles rose in silver stands, their flames moving as if underwater. Each flare threw shadows that organised themselves for a heartbeat into shapes, a rack of antlers, a river curling around a stone, the sweep of wings, then unravelled before my eyes could name them.

They sat at the far end.

Mom. Fiadh. My father.

Still, silent, dressed in black so dense it ate the light. Their faces were familiar until you looked at them too long. Then everything slipped. Skin too pale. Eyes too wide. A gaze that never blinked. Not human watching. The kind of watching that weighs and marks and waits to claim.

“Mom?” My voice cracked in the height.

Her mouth opened, but the answer came layered, older than throats, resonant like a note struck inside stone.

"You shine too brightly, little one."

The sentence pressed into my ribs from the inside. Not new, not remembered, like a lullaby once hissed at the edge of sleep in a language my bones knew and my mind did not.

Flames rose. Shadows stretched like reaching hands.

I felt him before I saw him. Heat moved across my skin in a low ribbon, curling under my stomach. My nerves fired like struck metal. Behind me, pressure gathered, not a touch yet, only certainty made into air.

"You always find your way back to me," he murmured at my ear, soft as a knife drawn slow from a sheath.

His hands slid to my hips as if they lived there, hot palms closing and pulling me into the hard brace of his body. My spine bowed, my shoulders set, my muscles gave without instruction. I hated that I breathed out relief.

"You should not be here," I managed.

"I belong wherever you come undone."

His lips skimmed the shell of my ear, barely contact, yet heat tracked the line he did not quite touch. The weight of him pressed against the small of my back, thick and deliberate. The dream had mass. He did.

"You are trembling."

"I should not want this."

"But you do."

His right hand travelled up my stomach, open palm warming the skin in a slow ascent until he cupped my breast. His thumb worked the nipple until it peaked hard enough to ache. Breath left me in small, broken pieces. At the far end of the table my family did not blink.

Everything was wrong. It should have cauterised any hunger it met. Instead, my body answered like a string struck in perfect tune.

"You have carried this hunger since you were a child," he said, voice deepening, edges roughening. "Even after they tried to erase it."

"My mother, "

"Your mother was never meant to sever us." His mouth brushed the shallow at the base of my throat. "Mnemosyne can bury memory, but she cannot unweave a thread already tied."

He turned me with an ease that told my muscles they had always obeyed him. I faced him fully. Those eyes burned like star maps folding inward. Fingers closing at my hips, he walked me back until the table's edge pressed cold into my thighs. The figures at the far end tracked each step. I felt their regard like cold breath on the back of my neck.

“No,” I said, shaking my head because it was the only thing I could control. “Not here.”

“You belong to me.”

The words struck and melted into me as if they had been written under my skin all along. He lifted me onto the table. Cold silk shocked my bare backs of thighs, then his warmth smothered it, thick and dizzying as heat after winter.

“Open,” he said.

The command did not need to be loud. My knees fell apart. He took my ankles in his hands and set them wide on the cloth. My sex throbbed at the naked exposure to candlelight and cold air. Shame rode the heat, sharp as nettles. I could not decide if it was punishment or proof.

“They are watching,” I whispered, because I had to mark that fact, place it in the air where I could see it.

“They have always known.” He lowered to his knees. “Your blood sings, Little Star. The stars live under your skin.”

His hands slid up the insides of my thighs, thumbs pressing, not rough yet, not kind either, a claim written in pressure.

Cold kissed my skin. I glanced down and saw the glint of steel. The knife hadn’t been there a moment before, conjured it straight into his hand, long and thin, the edge humming faint in the candlelight.

"Taz.." My voice broke, but he was already lowering it, slow, deliberate, until the blade lay flat across my thigh. The metal was cold enough to sting, the weight of it sharper for how steady his hand was.

"You tremble," he murmured, eyes locked on mine. "But you won't pull away."

He drew the knife's tip in a shallow line along the soft flesh high on my thigh, just deep enough for fire to flare under the skin. I gasped, hips jolting, but the sound that left me was want, not protest. Blood welled in a thin, bright ribbon.

Before I could speak, he bent and licked it. So slowly. His tongue traced the mark as if he were drinking the truth out of me. My thighs shook, shame and heat fusing until I couldn't tell them apart.

"Now you carry me," he said, voice raw with hunger. "Even when you wake."

The knife vanished as though it had never existed. His hands gripped my thighs again, spreading me wide, and this time when his mouth came down, the sting of the mark still burned under the heat of his tongue. The cut, the lick, the ache, all of it folded into the rhythm of him eating me, claim layered on claim until I couldn't separate pain from pleasure.

The first stroke of his tongue was ruinous. Hot, slow, the exact pace my body did not yet admit to wanting. He licked me from entrance to clit in a single long line and my spine came off the table on a sound I did not recognise as mine.

The hall caught the wet, obscene rhythm of him eating me and threw it back at us, softer, as if the room was careful not to scare me from the edge it wanted me on. He worked with vicious patience, the long strokes that wet everything, the smaller circles that made my thighs tremble, the precise flutter of the tip against the place that made my whole vision granulate into light.

"You taste like you were made for me," he said into me, the vibration flattening me to the cloth.

I gripped his hair the way a drowning person grips anything that will bear weight. He made a sound against me, pleased, and angled me higher over his mouth. The candlelight surged. Shadows ran up the walls in constellations and broke. I could not tell if that was the room or me.

"Look at me," he said.

I forced my head forward. He held my stare from between my thighs, eyes night-deep and greedy, tongue working me in slick, ruthless patterns that turned my bones to water. The humiliation of it welded itself to the need. I felt the shame and the relief at once, and it did something awful and exquisite to the inside of my ribs.

"You are breaking for me," he rasped, breath hot on my clit, then sealed his mouth over it and sucked.

The orgasm built like a storm shuddering above the city, electricity crawling the length of my limbs. I was there, Ready.,

He stopped.

He hovered a hair's breadth away. He breathed against me, name-shaped but not spoken.

"Please," I said, and hated that I sounded obedient.

"Shall I tell you what your mother never dared?"

Terror and want twisted until I could not tell which one made the noise that came out of me. "Please."

"The man who raised you was never your father."

The sentence went through me like glass. My body seized around the absence of his mouth. Pleasure shattered into bright, agonised fragments that cut and did not resolve.

"You shine because your true father was never mortal."

Tears stung. The held edge trembled just beyond reach, a wire I could not cross. "Who?"

His smile was slow, almost fond. He ran his hands up over my hips, held me open, and lowered his mouth again.

"Soon," he said into me.

The shock turned to anger, which turned to heat, which turned to need so intense it frightened me. He punished me for that, or rewarded it, I could not tell. His tongue moved with new intent, the drag and curl that locked me into a rhythm I could not escape, his jaw working as if he meant to keep me for himself from the inside. I tried to run from it, a useless scrabble against silk. He flattened my pelvis with a palm and kept me where he wanted me.

"Goddess," he said when my thighs shook. "Stay open."

"Please," I said again, this time a plea I did not dress in any other word.

He changed the angle and I came apart.

The climax tore through me like a star collapsing. Sound left my mouth without my consent. Muscles locked around his face, my feet pushing at his shoulders then pulling him closer, closer, as if I could make him part of me permanently if I held him hard enough. He did not stop. He took everything, licked me through the pulses until the long aftershocks ricocheted and broke again.

"That's it," he said against me, almost gentle now. "That is mine."

When the world returned, it did so in pieces, candle by candle. He rose over me and braced a hand beside my head. His mouth shone. He licked me from his lips with the same slow patience he had used to take me apart and looked pleased with the ruin he had made.

"You are mine, Goddess," he said, and the words cracked open the place inside me that had always been waiting to hear them.

He did not kiss me. He did not have to. The hall shifted its weight. Far away at the end of the table the three figures did not move, but something about their stillness changed. Agreement, perhaps. Or disappointment. I could not read their faces now. They were only masks for something larger.

I swallowed. "Tell me who."

"You are so close," he said, more promise than answer. His hand slid to my throat, not squeezing, only settling there, warm, definite, a collar made of skin and heat. He felt my swallow under his palm. He smiled like I had obeyed a command I did not hear.

"Say you will come back," he said.

"I will," I said, because I already knew I was lost.

The feast winked out as if the hall took a breath in and forgot to exhale. Dark fell. I fell with it.

I woke in my bed with the sheets damp under me, my pulse pounding so hard I could hear it in the pipes. Tears rolled over my temples into my hair. My thighs still ached with the shape of his mouth. I pressed my hand to my chest and felt the beat answer the word he had not said.

The truth sat in me like a living thing.

My father was not my father.

And I was not who I had been told I was.

Taz

She wakes gasping, the way drowning people do when the sea spits them back.

The sheets twist around her legs. Sweat slicks her skin in the hollow of her throat and at the bend of her knees. Her eyes are glass-bright and unfocused. No one has ever looked more beautiful to me than she does in the first half minute after I let her go.

I watch from the edge of the mirror. Not the reflection she pretends is safe. The other one. The layer of glass that remembers me. She does not look at it long. Some animal part of her recognises the wrongness and names it with my name without admitting that she has done so.

Her hand goes to her mouth. She touches her lower lip as if she can still feel me there. She can. Dreams leave taste when the dreamer belongs to the right god. She does. She always has.

I let her stay in the tremor. Thighs still parted. Belly rising and falling as if she cannot quite find enough air. Tears that are not only shame, not even mostly shame. Grief. Confusion. The sudden, terrifying relief of being given what she has needed for years without knowing the word for it.

That relief is mine. I fed it to her. I will feed it again.

Already the story they forced on her begins to unravel. The father they placed in the role begins to fade at the edges. She will tug at the loose threads now. She will tell herself she is only checking, only making sure. She will pretend she is in control of the unpicking. I will help her. Every doubt she nourishes is a pull on the cord that winds her back to me.

Fiadh thinks she is warning. She holds the shape of a cautionary tale and believes she is useful. She is not without use. A witness is a marker on a road. But she cannot sever what was bound before either of them learned the words for binding.

The real blood in Róisín sings to me every time she closes her eyes. Titan thread. Constellation woven through marrow. The taste of it is like honey set alight. Addictive in a way nothing mortal can imitate. The others would have reached for her if I had not found her first. Perhaps they tried. They did not hold on as I did.

I found her small and star-eyed, nine years old, stepping barefoot into the white like someone who has never been taught to fear thresholds. She carried light cupped in her hands and did not yet know that gifts given in dreams write contracts deeper than law. She offered it. I took it. That is the beginning. Everything after is a consequence of that first exchange.

Mnemosyne tore her from me. She used the old knife and cut the thread and salted the cut with forgetting. I walked empty rooms for years that smelled like her hair and the sea and the laugh the dome loved. I touched every wall in the places we had made and did not speak because the only thing I had to say was her name and it had been burned out of the air.

But coffins rot. Doors swell and warp. Memory is tide. Tide returns.

Now she breathes me again without meaning to. Resistance is a tether by another name. Pull against the cord and all you do is keep the line tight.

I could step out of the glass tonight. I could lay my weight along her spine and hold her wrists above her head and take her until there is nothing left in her mouth but my name. It would be easy to make a cathedral of this bed and an altar of her body. It would be mercy to both of us.

But I will not. Not yet.

The next knot must be tied by her hands. She must say yes with the same mouth that has said no, and mean it, and then she will be mine in a way even Mnemosyne will not try to break again. When the truth about her father slides fully into the light, when she accepts that she is the child of divinity and shadow and not the man they placed at the table of her life, she will come into my arms by choice.

She will understand that I am the only one who has not lied to her.

When she comes, I will take her apart patiently and put her back together in my shape. I will burn every borrowed touch out of her skin. I will mark her so that any creature who looks on her in any world, waking or dreaming, will know she belongs to me.

The spiral turns.

I have waited years that felt like continents.

I can wait a little longer.

Chapter Twenty-One

Phantom Fire
Róisín & Taz

Roisin

The mirror pulsed behind the scarf.

I did not touch it. I did not need to. The air changed the way air changes before thunder. A hush that was not quiet. A weight that pressed lightly first, then with intention, as if a hand were resting against the other side of the glass.

Watching. Breathing. Waiting.

The dream still lived under my skin, a low ember lodged between my hips, heat coiled and patient, refusing to cool. Every step reminded me of his mouth. Every blink replayed his voice.

The man who raised you was never your father.

It had split something open in me. A seam I had kept stitched for years came apart with one sentence and a tongue on my clit. I tried to sew it shut with logic and failed. I tried to hold still and the ground moved anyway.

I was breaking. Worse, I was starting to want to break.

The lab was heavier today. Or I was. Light sat on everything like frost, bright and thin, making edges too sharp. The hum from the banks of machines had picked up a pitch just high enough to scratch along the inside of my skull. I could feel it in my teeth. My temples pulsed in an off rhythm, a second heartbeat that did not belong to me. The world bent at its own borders when I turned my head too quick, as if a hidden layer kept trying to peel back and show itself.

Jamie was waiting at my desk, pretending not to be.

"Ro," he said, soft enough that I had to step closer. "You missed calibration. Again."

"I rescheduled."

"You don't reschedule."

He eased into my space like a tide coming in. Not sudden. Persistent. "You cannot keep pretending nothing is happening."

The words snagged on something I did not want to name. He saw my stillness and took it as permission, or invitation, or victory. His fingers drifted over my forearm. The touch was light and testing, a probe pressed to a bruise to find its shape.

"You are tired," he went on. "You are slipping. You will not let anyone steady you."

"I do not need you."

His mouth curled. Not friendly. The patience of a man happy to wait for prey to stumble.

"You will," he said, and then he lowered his voice further, a velvet drop into something intimate that made my skin crawl. "You are seeing him again, are you not?"

Blood left my face so fast I thought I might faint. The quick freeze of it gave me away. He watched me like a man watching numbers settle on a screen.

"I can see it," he murmured. "In the way you move now. In your face."

"You do not know what you are talking about."

"You cannot hide it, Ro." His eyes warmed in the particular way that is not warmth at all. "You want something you should not. Something dangerous."

For a sharp second I saw my hand rise and slap him. The imagined sound was sweet and bright. I did not move. I would not give him a story he could own.

"You do not know anything," I said, because my voice would not give me a better sentence.

He smiled as if he did not require my belief. "I know enough. And when you finally fall apart, I will still be here."

I turned away before my rage became action and let the elevator doors close between us like a mouth shutting on my tongue.

Outside, the city felt thinner, like skin stretched over bone. Streetlights buzzed like insects. Puddles shivered without feet to disturb them. My reflection in a shopfront was wrong for a second, too tall and too still, as if I were a cut-out pasted onto the scene.

Sometimes it was not me at all.

In the warped black glass of a café window, a shape stood where my shoulder should have been. The impossible height. The angle of a jaw I knew by feel now. The suggestion of eyes that held night like a held breath.

I blinked.

Gone.

My pussy pulsed at nothing. At memory. At the suggestion of him in the world where he was not meant to be. Shame tangled with a quick, hot ache that felt like a bruise thumbed on purpose. I was craving him awake now. The border between sleeping and not sleeping had thinned until it felt like lace.

The mirror at home breathed when I crossed the threshold. The scarf trembled once as if a draft had found it, though the windows were shut. I did not look directly at the glass. I set the spiral-covered book by the couch and knelt on the rug like a person about to pray and did not pray.

The air thickened. Warmer now. Charged.

I felt him. Not in the way a thought feels. In the way a presence rearranges a room. The back of my neck prickled. Phantom heat pressed along my spine and held.

"You are here," I whispered.

His voice poured into my ear like dark silk licking a blade. "I am always here."

My nipples hardened under the thin cotton of my shirt. Sensation tightened down the back of my legs and into my arches. I pressed my thighs together and the ache answered by blooming wider.

"Stop," I said, because the part of me that keeps lists needed the word on the record. "You should not be here."

"But you want me here."

Tears sprung sudden and surprised into my eyes. My hand slid under the hem of my shirt without asking me first. Trembling as if I were cold. I was not.

"No."

"Yes."

A breath like a mouth grazed the place where my pulse beats in my neck. The nerve there jumped and ran through me like a wire pulled tight. Heat spread under my skin in lines.

"Touch yourself for me."

The sentence dropped through me and hit the floor. I caught myself with my own hand. I circled my clit once, a light test, then again, firmer, because the first touch did not answer the ache. My hips rose into my fingers like they had been waiting for the signal. My breathing broke into quick, shallow pulls I could not slow.

"You were made for me," he said, voice threaded with something old enough to make the room feel smaller. "You carry starlight in your blood. My Little Star."

A noise shivered out of me. Not a word. A sound with more heat than sense.

"You do not own me," I said, and meant it in the same breath that failed me.

"I always have."

"Say please," I said, sudden, reckless, because some part of me wanted him to meet me where I was still fighting.

Silence thickened like honey. His answer stroked the inside of my skull.

"Please. Spread yourself."

My knees softened. I slid two fingers through my own slick and opened myself with a heat-humiliated sigh. He did not need to be here to hold my wrists. He was here anyway.

"Good," he said. "Circle. Slow. Count."

"One," I breathed, and circled. "Two. Three."

"Slower."

I obeyed. I hated the word and the way my body took it in like a sweet.

"Four," I whispered, and the rhythm found me, a patient draw of skin over nerve.

"Do not chase it," he said. "Let it come to you."

I tried. I failed. I chased. He laughed, quiet and pleased, and the sound made my toes curl into the rug.

"Again," he said. "Count."

I counted until numbers blurred. He set the pace with a word when I went too fast, and with a breath when I hesitated. He did not touch me and he touched me everywhere. He fed me the command I did not know I wanted.

"Say my name," he said.

I bit the sound off. My hips wanted to offer it. My mouth did not.

"Then cum without it."

The order slid under the shame and hooked into something older than either. The orgasm rose hard and bright. I asked for him where he could not hear. He heard anyway.

"Now," he said.

I broke. I bit my own hand to catch the noise, but it still got out, a ragged cry dragged through my teeth. My body convulsed around my fingers. Aftershocks rolled long and slow, sweet and cruel, and I let them take me until the world softened at the edges again.

When I could breathe without it snagging, I rolled onto my side and faced the mirror. The scarf hung obedient and dull. No light bled from the edges. No shape leaned. I knew better than what my eyes said.

"Goddess," he said in the dark that was not empty.

I wanted to be angry. I wanted to be sick. I wanted to climb into the glass and be done with the space between.

I slept where I fell.

Taz

She believes she is still resisting.

Tonight she touched herself for me with her eyes open. Not dreaming. Not bound by rules I make. Awake, kneeling, obedient to a command she asked me to give.

The barrier thins. The thread tightens. I can taste the starlight in her blood from this side of the glass, sweet as fruit stolen at night. The rooms I built for her have taught her language from the inside out. White corridors, forests that breathe, cathedrals that hum her name, halls set for feasts of knowing. All of that so that when I finally told her to open, her body would hear the instruction and call it home.

She counted for me tonight. She asked, and I gave, and she obeyed. Not because I forced her. Because the hunger has remembered its own mouth.

She is close. The last of the forgetting sits like frost at the edge of a field and the sun is up. When it burns, there will be no more walls that hold. No more waking that protects. Only us and the rooms I will make.

I can wait. I can also take. The pleasure of patience is how it sharpens the taking.

Róisín

The street outside the lab wore that pale evening Galway keeps for itself, the light that drags colour out of everything and leaves only shape. In the corner of my vision something golden darted across the pavement, thin as a ribbon of sun breaking through a cloud. I turned quick enough to make a passer-by glance back.

Nothing. Just concrete and my own long shadow stretched thin by a streetlamp.

By the time I reached my building, I had told myself it was fatigue or blood sugar or wishful thinking. I set my bag on the chair, reached for my journal on the shelf, meaning to record clean facts before they smudged.

The leather burned my palms.

Not scorch. Not sensation at the surface. A deep, slow heat that rolled up through the meat of my hands as if the book held a coal and I had held the coal too long. I dropped it. It hit the rug with a fat sound and lay there accusing the air.

The heat dulled to a throb. When I looked down, shapes had risen in pale gold under the skin. Not random blotches. Not heat rash. A small sun at the centre of each palm, fine lines radiating out like a star drawn with care and a compass. They shimmered when I tilted them, then settled when I held still.

I did not touch the journal again.

Later, as the kettle started its small coughs, a voice slipped through the kitchen wall, a man speaking low to someone I could not hear.

"…keep her cold."

The kettle clicked to finished, loud enough to end the line. I pressed my ear to the paint. Nothing but the mutter of a television a floor down and the lift complaining as it moved.

Steam curled from the spout like a hand with no owner. My palms still tingled with faint heat, like I had been stamped at the door to a place I had not agreed to enter.

I drank my tea black and too hot and did not taste it.

The mirror in the hall held its breath behind the scarf. I stood in front of it and did not lift the cloth. I imagined the marks on my hands shining on the other side and felt a small, wild urge to see. I did not move. I stood there until the skin between my shoulder blades crawled.

In bed, the city pressed its noise through the gaps in the window seal. A gull cried as if it were a person who had lost a name. Somewhere a siren ran down a street that did not lead to me. I lay on my back and stared at the ceiling and promised myself I would sleep without him.

Warmth gathered low like a hand cupped over a candle. A breath touched my throat from the wrong direction.

“Say please,” I whispered into the dark, and hated how fast the word arrived.

The answer was immediate and patient and full of certainty.

“Please,” he said. “Come back.”

Chapter Twenty-Two

The Echoes of Her Name

Róisín & Taz

Roisin

Reality was losing its edges.

It wasn't only the dreams anymore. It was the way the lights stuttered when I swiped into the lab, fluorescent tubes hiccupping like nerves. It was the hum of the EEG banks, no longer a soft blanket of white noise but pitched and deliberate, a thread pulled tight and dragged across the inside of my skull. It was voices lagging a half-beat behind mouths, a syllable out of step, as if sound itself was slipping on the tiles and righting itself a fraction too late.

And I saw it in the patients.

Patient 056 was deep in REM when it happened. The room had that held-breath hush I usually love: the gentle metronome of the pulse ox, the slow rise and fall of the chest, the small sounds machines make when they're behaving. Order. Predictability. A steady descent along the architecture of sleep.

Then her EEG leapt like a deer startled in traffic, clean curve shattering into angry jag, jag, jag, as if the line itself were splintering the longer it ran. The monitor didn't freeze; it convulsed. Not a simple buffer stutter. A seizure of data, an intrusion that forced the feed to make room.

At first there was only breath on the audio channel. Then the faintest scrape of syllables, as if someone were learning how to speak inside her throat.

"Róisín…"

My name.

His voice.

The intern beside me straightened, headphones pushed more firmly to her ears. She glanced at me, unsure, excitement and discomfort fighting behind her eyes. On screen, the wave spiralled, a perfect coil blooming, tightening, blooming again in time with the patient's heart.

"Did you, "

"Artifact," I said, too sharp, a cut rather than an explanation. "Audio glitch."

But the shape wasn't a glitch. The spiral pulsed with her pulse and then with mine. I felt the second beat arrive in my own chest, the way a second shadow stands beside yours at noon. I swallowed and it swallowed with me.

It's spreading.

By mid-afternoon, it had infected everything. The files on my desktop sprouted corrupted margins like fungus. Symbols crept into the metadata, the same angles I'd been drawing in the corners of my notebooks without meaning to. The spiral etched itself into the graphs as if the programme had always contained it. My own name appeared in broken loops inside filenames I hadn't touched yet.

My skin itched under my clothes. My nipples tightened against the cheap cotton of my bra. Panic crawled slow up my throat even as something lower pulsed in steady time, insistent, shameless. I was wide awake. He was here. Always here.

I tried to move through the day by ritual: kettle on, mugs counted, clipboards stacked, laces tied and retied, pens aligned in a row. The small order I could make and keep. It didn't hold. The air had thickened in the corridors; it tasted faintly metallic, like heat before lightning.

I was heading to the archive when Jamie appeared out of the stillness like a thought I didn't want to think. He had that practised look again. The one he imagines is care because it wears the right face.

"Ro," he said.

"Jesus, Jamie." My voice came out brittle.

He kept coming, closer than the hallway allowed. The corridor here was always a little colder than the rest, sealed too well, the kind of place where you can hear your own mouth open. His eyes had that gleam again, the one that feels like concern until you realise it's curiosity with a soft tone.

"You need to stop this," he said quietly. "You need to let go of whatever you think is happening."

"You don't know what you're talking about."

"I know exactly what's happening."

His hand shot out, faster than I expected, fingers closing around my arm above the wrist. Not the polite grip of a colleague. A seal. Hard enough that I'd wear his shape tomorrow.

"You're breaking," he said, and his voice shifted. A register lower. Something hiding under the vowels. "And if you fall into him, you won't come back."

The air altered as if the corridor had inhaled. A pressure change, faint then obvious. The shadows behind him brightened and darkened in a slow pulse, as if they'd learned to breathe. Heat rolled over my skin in a deep, patient wave that stood the hair on my arms. I felt my own mouth part in answer.

He's here.

Jamie's head snapped up towards the ceiling like an animal scenting.

"You were never supposed to wake," he growled, and the growl wasn't his.

Mnemosyne. A leash. A plant. A failsafe dressed like a man with good intentions and a decent haircut. I saw the line for what it was and bile rose hot behind my tongue.

"Let me go," I said.

He didn't.

The lights above us cracked like thin ice stepped on without care. Glass powdered into the air; the corridor plunged into a flickering half-dark. The emergency strips along the skirting board shone a mean green. Ozone bit the back of my throat. The glass door at the end of the hall shimmered, the panel turning liquid, the reflection bending into a lens.

And then he was there.

Not a trick of light. Not a shiver of suggestion.

Taz.

Full and solid in the glass, as if the door had learned depth and he occupied it. Galaxies burning slow in his eyes, constellations tightening, his mouth curled in a snarl of hunger threaded with fury.

The surface bulged outward as if a chest were pressing against it from the other side. The heat hit first, not the slap of a summer day but a deep heat. It slammed into Jamie and flung him into the wall with a sound I felt in my teeth. He slid to the floor, breath gone to nothing, shock blooming across his face.

I staggered back, a hand over my sternum as if I could keep my ribs from unbuttoning. The glass breathed once more and then held. Taz's gaze locked to mine through the distance and through the impossible. The words filled me without crossing the air.

No one touches what's mine.

The letters vibrated against my bones, a tuning fork struck in the centre of me. I couldn't move. Couldn't breathe. Terror ran hot and clean, and with it something dirtier and more honest that sat low and pulsed. We looked at each other like the only two animals left in a world made of glass.

The door stilled. The surface flattened. The emergency strips steadied. Overhead, one remaining tube flickered and then surrendered, humming itself back to life.

Jamie made a small, ugly sound as his breath returned. He dragged himself to his knees and used the wall to stand, eyes on the floor, mouth working around a swallow he hadn't earned.

I clutched my chest and tried to take a full breath. It came in sharp pieces. I didn't know what scared me more. That Jamie had been placed here to manage me like a hazard. Or that Taz had reached for me in waking and the world had bent.

His eyes held mine through the glass. His mouth didn't move.

Run.

The word landed like a push between my shoulder blades. I moved without thought, feet buffering the floor in quick, soft slaps, past Jamie, past the lift, down the service stairs that smelled of bleach and old rain. I didn't stop until the back door banged behind me and the evening air put its cold hands on my face.

I didn't stop then either.

I ran until the city slowed me. Until the dock appeared at the end of a street and the water said *enough* in the way water says everything. I bent over with my hands on my knees and counted breaths like a child, one to five, five to one, until I could pretend I was the person whose breath belonged to this chest.

I did not go home. I walked. I let the tide keep time. I let shopfronts look back and chose not to look in. I bought a bottle of water and drank it too fast. I watched the reflected lights break across the surface of a puddle and pretended they were only electricity and not geography.

When I finally turned my key in my own door, the flat exhaled and made space for me. The scarf over the hall mirror hung obediently. The kettle clicked once, twice, as if reassuring me it still knew how to be a kettle. In the calm after a storm you can hear the damage you'll have to name in the morning. I stood and listened to the not-quite-silence and knew I didn't have a word for what had changed.

I undressed mechanically, not out of modesty, out of inventory. Clothes on chair, hair tied, water, pills, lamp, lock, check, check, check. My hands were steady enough to fool a stranger. They didn't fool me.

In bed, the ceiling looked higher than it had yesterday. I lay on my back and pretended my body wasn't tuned to a frequency I couldn't switch off.

"You will not come," I whispered to no one, and felt the heat answer from my own skin.

Sleep took me by the ankle and pulled.

Taz

I could have stepped through.

One more breath with my hands in the glass and the surface would have surrendered. I would have taken the thickness of the door into my palms and parted it the way a curtain parts for a king who never knocks. I would have stood in her corridor with heat in my hands and the curve of her throat under my fingers. I would have taken the sound from her mouth against mine, and the world would have learned a new way to hold us.

The leash Mnemosyne left in me burned bright as a brand. I did not care. It is easy to mistake pain for a boundary. It is a better discipline to step past it.

He had touched her.

That thin mortal thread of a man had wrapped his hand around my star and squeezed hard enough to bruise. I felt the mark bloom on her arm as if the skin were my own. I wanted to drag him through into my dark and lay him on a floor of cold stars and feed him to the places between the constellations, a scream at a time. Let him learn what a hand is for.

Her eyes found me. Wide and bright. Panic swimming in them, yes, but heat too, the quick startled heat I have coaxed from her in a thousand nights. The tether snapped tight, a cord pulled to its end, and the air in her corridor rounded with it, heavy with mine. My heat. My scent. My want. Her pulse jumped. Her thighs answered. Her breath broke and remade itself. Even here, even in the world that thinks it is immune to me, her body remembered me first.

She does not yet understand what I am. Or what I have made to find her again.

Every place she has wandered in her sleep I stitched from the remnants of our first world: the breathing trees, the drowning room, the cathedral that sings when I say her name, the feast set in a hall that remembers her mother's sentence and repeats it. They aren't just dreams. They are maps. Each chamber a path. Each path a finger laid on her back, pressing her toward the door with my mark on it.

I have been patient. I have let myself starve until hunger became holy. I have learned the pleasure that comes from denying what is easy so that the taking is clean.

There is more they have not told her. More than the story of a man who is not her father. More than the reasons a mother begged a Goddess to cut the thread that belonged to us. Her blood burns gold when the right light touches it. I have seen that fire once before in a boy grown into a man who held daylight in his hands and thought himself untouchable. I know what lineage does to a life.

Jamie is not an accident. He is a tether knotted to her ankle and hidden under the cuff of a lab coat. A leash disguised as loyalty. They think I did not notice the knot. They think a leash changes anything except the way a body marks when it pulls.

The glass shivered under my palms, the way a chest shivers under a sob you choose to swallow. The corridor's air pulled towards me. If I had called her, she would have crossed the distance with the honest obedience of a woman going to her name.

Not yet.

The next knot must be tied by her hand. She must say yes with the same mouth that has practiced no. She must bring her throat to my palm because she wants the weight of it there. When the truth of her father steps fully into her, when she finally sees the thread crowding under her skin for what it is, she will come by choice, and all the knives Mnemosyne carries won't cut what we make then.

So I gave her the only thing that would stay inside her after I left. A word she would hear when she lay in her bed with her hands folded on the sheet like a question.

Run.

I meant three things, and she will hear all of them when she thinks about what her legs did in that corridor.

Run now, before I break the glass and take you where there are no witnesses.

Run, because the man they placed behind you is still breathing and I will tear him down to the smallness he hides if he lays a hand on you again.

Run, because next time, Little Star, I will not stop.

The word left me and the door cooled under my skin. The leash eased from white to dull red. The corridor took its shape back. She moved like a deer that has seen the wolf and isn't sure whether to believe the tree will shelter it.

Let them think I did not step through because I could not. Let them sleep under that lie. I do not sleep.

The thread hums. The spiral turns.

She is running. She is also coming to me. Both can be true.

I wait with my hand open and the glass remembering the shape of it.

Chapter Twenty-Three

The Infinite Shore
Róisín & Taz

Roisin

I didn't fall asleep. I fell through.

The pull was instant, violent, the moment my eyelids closed, the weight of him wrapped around me, dragging me under like a current I could never escape.

The world bled into place in pieces.

Black water lapped against an endless, silver-edged shore, each wave moving as if pulled by a heartbeat older than time. The sky was not entirely black, constellations twisted in strange, impossible ways, stars bursting and bleeding across the void as if the heavens themselves were being torn apart. And beneath it all, the air hummed.

I stood barefoot at the edge of the water. Naked. Again.

The breeze was warm, tasting electric. My skin prickled, every nerve alive, waiting for what I knew would come.

I felt him before I saw him.

The air thickened. The sand shifted faintly beneath my feet. My own pulse answered like a drumbeat under my skin.

He stepped from the shadows behind me as if the shore had birthed him, massive, bare-chested, the galaxies in his eyes alive and shifting, their light swirling with something older than the stars themselves.

My throat tightened. My chest rose and fell too fast.

"You're shaking, Little Star." His voice was velvet over steel, sliding into me like it had always belonged there.

My nipples hardened instantly, the ache blooming low in my belly. I hated the way my body leaned toward him before I even turned.

"You've fought long enough," he breathed.

He moved in front of me, circling like a predator who already knew the outcome. His gaze mapped me slowly, reverently, as if taking inventory of every inch he'd been denied.

"You've carried the stars in your blood since birth," he murmured. "But you were always meant to burn for me."

The spiral spun faintly behind my eyes, a pulse that wasn't mine alone.

"I don't know who I am," I whispered.

"Yes, you do."

He closed the space between us until his breath brushed my lips.
"You're mine."

The words vibrated through me, all the way to the aching core of me. My knees weakened, but his arms were already there, lifting me effortlessly against his chest, cradling me like something both sacred and claimed.

"You feel it," he whispered into my hair. "The power waking in you."

My body trembled. My pulse roared in my ears.

"You were born of prophecy. Your mother's sky..." his hands slid slowly down my thighs, parting me as the warm water licked at our skin, "...and your father's fire."

I gasped, the sound breaking in my throat, as his fingers brushed the slick heat between my legs.

"But you'll burn for me."

His touch was slow, deliberate, maddening in its precision, circling, teasing, refusing to give me what I wanted until I pushed into his hand. My hips betrayed me, arching.

"Say it," he coaxed. "Say you're mine."

I shook my head, tears stinging my eyes, but my body pulsed around emptiness, desperate to be filled.

"You are mine, Róisín."

Two fingers slid into me, curling perfectly, like they'd been carved for this alone. My breath shattered. My walls gripped him greedily.

"You've always been mine."

He moved with unbearable patience, every thrust of his fingers tugging me closer to something inevitable. Above us, the constellations bent, rearranging themselves into shapes I almost remembered, a boy's laughter, my own small hands placing stars in patterns no mortal sky had ever held.

"You don't have to be afraid," he murmured. "I will take you."

The words broke me. "Yes," I gasped. "I want you."

"Louder."

"I want you."

"Goddess."

His fingers withdrew. My body protested, until his cock pressed against my entrance, hot, thick, perfect.

"Breathe for me."

He pushed inside in one long, slow thrust, forcing a cry from my throat. The stretch was dizzying, perfect, my pussy gripping him like he'd never been gone.

He stilled, letting me feel every inch of him. "You feel me now," he rasped. "You were made for this."

Then he began to move. Slow at first. Deliberate. Every deep grind into me stole my breath. The stars above flared brighter with each thrust. The waves licked my sides like worship.

"I want to watch you fall apart," he growled, and his pace quickened, forcing broken sounds from my throat.

My orgasm climbed fast, brutal. He caught my wrists, pinning them above my head, locking me under him completely.

"You're mine."

"I'm yours," I sobbed.

He fucked me through the first climax, relentless. The second ripped through me harder, the sky fracturing into light.

"You can take more."

The third hit like an explosion. My body convulsed, sobbing his name as the universe spun apart around us.

He came with a low growl, hips jerking as heat flooded deep inside me.

He stayed there, buried to the hilt, forehead pressed to mine as the cosmos above slowed, stars resettling into their places.

"You'll remember soon," he whispered. "All of it."

And I knew, this wasn't just sex. It was the reweaving of something ancient. And I was already lost.

Taz

I built the Infinite Shore for her.

Every grain of black sand, every fractured constellation bleeding across the sky, I chose them. She thinks the dream pulls her in by accident, but nothing here is accidental. Every detail is a thread, every thread is a snare.

I've been shaping this place for years. Mapping it in the quiet madness between her dreams, refining it until it hums with the exact pitch of her soul. She steps onto this shore and the world becomes a mirror of what she is, vast, ancient, dangerous.

She doesn't know yet that I've always been here. Even when she was nine. Even when Mnemosyne's leash yanked her away.

I see the girl she was in the set of her jaw when she tries to deny me, in the tilt of her head when she searches the sky for patterns she doesn't remember placing. She doesn't know the constellations above us are the ones we made together, years before she knew what wanting was.

She was supposed to be mine first. I should have been her first kiss, her first taste, her first breaking. They took that from me. From us.

Now I'll take everything else.

When I touch her, I'm not just fucking her, I'm burning through the last of Mnemosyne's bindings, unravelling the walls they built in her mind. Every shudder, every cry, every clench of her pussy around me loosens the knot they tied to keep me out.

She thinks the orgasms are hers alone, a gift I'm giving her. They're not. They're keys.

I watch her unravel beneath me, the stars above us spinning into the patterns we drew as children. The sky bends to the rhythm of her body, each climax sending shockwaves through the dream until the whole shore vibrates with her.

She tells me she wants me, finally says it, and my control almost breaks. I could take her harder. Push until she forgets her name and all she knows is mine. But there's still more she has to remember before I let her shatter completely.

When I spill inside her, it isn't release. It's a seal.

A mark that will follow her into waking, warm and aching, no matter how she tries to scrub it away.

I hold her there, forehead to forehead, letting her feel my breath as the tide retreats. I could tell her the rest now, about Apollo, about the prophecy that makes her blood worth more than empires, about how every moment of her life has been bent toward this night.

But not yet.

If I told her now, she might run for the wrong reasons. When she runs, I want it to be because she finally knows what it means to be mine.

So I let her go. For now.

Chapter Twenty-Four

Residual Heat

Roisin

I woke soaked in sweat.

The heat clung to me like a second skin, damp and suffocating. My sheets were tangled around my legs, plastered to my thighs in a way that made me shiver even as I burned. My breath came in short, shallow bursts, the kind you make when you're trying not to cry or trying not to come.

Every part of me felt wrecked. My pussy throbbed, sore and swollen from how violently I'd broken apart in the dream. My muscles ached in that delicious, humiliating way that follows being taken too long, too hard. My limbs felt loose and boneless, but underneath, my nerves hummed, sharp, electric, like something was still inside me.

Because something was.

I sat up slowly, the sheets dragging against my sensitised skin, and pressed my palm between my legs. The flesh there was tender, fever-warm. I could almost *cup* the ghost of him, feel the thick weight of him still holding me open, stretching me. The dream had dissolved, but the mark of him hadn't.

The spiral burned behind my eyes. *You're mine.*

His voice was still there, deep and intimate, as if his mouth was against my ear. Close. Always close now.

But beneath the heat and hunger, there was something else. A stillness inside my chest. Coiled. Waiting. Like a bowstring drawn tighter and tighter but not yet loosed.

⋆ ★ · ⋆ · ★ · ⋆ · ★

The world outside felt wrong.

The air was heavier. Brighter. Edges too sharp. Colours too saturated, as if my eyes were registering something they hadn't before. People moved past me on the pavement, wrapped in their own lives, but their eyes lingered, half a second too long.

A child in a stroller met my gaze and burst into tears.

A crow landed on a lamppost as I passed, glossy feathers drinking in the light. It cawed once, sharp, tilting its head as if memorising my face.

The pull between my ribs hadn't stopped since I woke. A constant thread, tugging me toward something I couldn't see but could *feel.*

I was different now.

And I didn't know if that meant I should be terrified… or hungry.

⋆ ⋆ · ⋆ · ⋆ · ⋆ ⋆

At the lab, the glitches were worse.

EEG logs flickered in and out, segments replaced with corrupted static. In the margins of my files, fractal spirals bloomed in neat black lines, symbols I didn't remember typing. My own name appeared in places it didn't belong, embedded like code that had always been there.

Jamie wasn't in today. For once. That made it worse.

Siobhán caught me by the breakroom, her coffee cooling in her hands. "Hey," she said, hesitating. "Have you been feeling… weird?"

I forced a neutral blink. "Define weird."

She stepped closer, voice dropping. "The equipment's been spiking all week. Audio glitches. Subjects saying things in their sleep that aren't in the scripts."

A quiet, cold thread worked its way down my spine. "Like what?"

Her gaze darted toward the hallway before she answered. "Someone said your name again this morning. Clear as anything. Another whispered about stars… and keys."

I swallowed. My stomach felt hollow. "Just contamination. Suggestibility," I said, too fast. "We've seen it before."

Siobhán didn't look convinced. "Maybe. But it feels… different this time. Like something's building." She searched my face, her tone softening. "Are you okay, Ro?"

No. Because I could feel him *behind me*. Right then. Close enough that the fine hairs at my nape rose, the air warmer where his presence touched it.

I managed a small, empty smile. "I'm fine."

She didn't push, but I felt her eyes on me long after she left.

That night, the pull inside me tightened until I couldn't ignore it.

I sat cross-legged on the floor beside the covered mirror, the spiral-covered book open in my lap. The pages smelled faintly of smoke and rain.

The air shifted. Warmth rolled over my bare arms, a slow tide. *You feel it now, don't you?*

"Yes," I breathed.

The heat of him pressed into my back, invisible, but so *real*. I could feel where his thighs would cage mine if he were solid, where his hands would grip my hips to keep me from moving away.

You're waking.

I bit my lip. "There's more I don't know."

There's much you don't know.

His voice was different now, reverent, almost gentle, though it coiled with that same hunger. *You carry your mother's stars,* he whispered, *but your father's fire pulses beneath your skin.*

I gasped, the sound breaking from me like something pulled loose. "Tell me who he is."

Not yet, Little Star.

The warmth curled closer, his mouth almost brushing the edge of my ear. My whole body went tight.

But you will remember.

The spiral spun hard and fast behind my eyes. My thighs pressed together without thought, the ache between them blooming sharp and shameful.

"You used me," I whispered.

I claimed what was always mine.

The pulse in my pussy throbbed at the words, my body betraying me again.

"You love me," I gasped.

With every breath I exist.

"Then why…" my voice cracked, "why does this feel like something else?"

His silence was heavy, like a hand closing around my throat.

Above me, in the black of my mind, the stars were spinning faster, pulling into new shapes.

I could feel it now, the change in my bones, in my blood, in something vast and ancient inside me I had never touched before.

And whatever was coming…

It wasn't done breaking me. Not yet.

Chapter Twenty-Five

The Key of Glass
Roisin & Taz

Roisin

It began with a memory I didn't remember having.

A burst of light. Gold. Blinding. The kind of brightness that felt *alive*, that seared my eyes but didn't hurt. It kissed every nerve until I could taste it on my tongue, a strange mingling of heat and honey, and under it, something metallic, like the moment before lightning strikes.

And a voice. Deep, resonant. So certain it made my ribs ache, as if the words had been carved into me before I was born.

"You were born of prophecy, little one. Light will always find you."

I woke with a gasp that tore my throat raw. My heart pounded so hard it felt like my ribs were straining to hold it in. Sweat plastered my nightshirt to my back, my hair damp and curling at my temples. My chest burned, a slow, steady ache, as if someone had placed a sun behind my sternum and left it there to pulse.

My fingertips tingled. My mouth tasted of copper.

The spiral pulsed behind my eyes, no longer distant or hazy. Tighter now. Sharper. Insistent.

I stumbled out of bed, pacing the room like an animal too aware of its cage. My breathing came fast and shallow. Every inhale felt too small. There was *something* inside me, clawing for release, something old, something bright, something that did not belong entirely to me.

The house felt wrong. Or maybe I did.

I tore through the closet, my hands clumsy, catching on cardboard flaps and paper edges. Boxes split open, spilling my past onto the floor, books, loose photographs, folded letters in my mother's handwriting, curling with age.

At the very bottom, under dust and time, I found it. A leather-wrapped journal I didn't recognise.

It wasn't hers. The weight of it felt deliberate. Like it had been waiting for *me* specifically.

The first page was blank. The second held a single inscription in perfect, deliberate script:

To my daughter. The key is within you. When you remember his light, you will understand who you are.

Beneath the words, a spiral, but not the one I knew. This one was crowned in tiny, precise sunbursts, each point radiating outward in perfect symmetry.

Not just stars. Light.

The truth struck me like a physical blow. Apollo.

Not just starlight. Not just dreams. Prophecy.

My breath hitched, sharp and shallow, as the world seemed to narrow to that page.

"*My Goddess.*"

His voice. Close enough to make the hairs rise along my arms.

My throat tightened. "You knew."

"Of course I knew."

"You needed me to break so you could pull my power forward."

"I needed you to awaken."

The phantom heat of him pressed in from behind, dragging invisible fingers up my spine with aching slowness.

"Your surrender isn't only mine, Little Star. Your surrender unlocks what sleeps inside you."

My chest heaved. "You used me."

"I loved you."

The words landed sharp, cutting deeper than I wanted to admit.

"And I will love you when you burn brighter than you ever imagined."

My voice cracked. "What do you want from me?"

"Everything."

The mirror pulled at me then.
Not just calling, *summoning*.

The scarf slipped from it with a whisper, pooling at my feet.

The glass shimmered faintly beneath my palm, vibrating into my bones. And there, ghosting across its surface, was the spiral crowned in sunbursts, the same as in the journal.

Not just a mirror. A lock.

And I… was the key.

"When you open it, you open me."

"Are you trapped?"

"You know I am."

"Is that why you needed me to break?"

"You were always the door."

The truth hollowed me out and filled me all at once. He didn't just *want* me. He needed me.
To free himself.
To cross into the waking world.
To claim everything.

And still… my hands shook with want. My thighs pressed together, heat blooming so fiercely between them it was humiliating.

A hairline crack split across the glass beneath my fingertips. The sound was sharp. Alive.

⋆ ⋆ · ⋆ · ⋆ · ⋆ ˙ ⋆

Taz

I felt it.

The moment her fingers touched the glass, it hit me like lightning splitting stone. The first fracture.

Not in the mirror, in the boundary itself.

It's been centuries since I felt a breach this real. The sensation nearly dropped me to my knees. The walls between our worlds groaned, strained. For the first time in far too long, I could *taste* the air of hers.

And I know I wasn't the only one. Mnemosyne will have stirred. She'll feel the lock weakening. She'll know her leash is slipping.

Good. Let her fucking come.

She doesn't understand what she's done.

She doesn't know the light in that false memory wasn't mine. That the voice she heard, *the one that told her light will always find her*, belongs to the one I've been waiting to take from the start.

Apollo. Her true father. Her bloodline. Her fire.

It doesn't matter. Stars or sunlight, they burn the same when I claim them.

The crack will spread now. Every touch, every dream, every time her pulse stutters for me, it will widen.

And I can already feel her heat through it, not the pale, tentative longing of those first nights, but something deeper. Hungrier. Her thighs clenching, her pussy wet for me before I've even spoken her name. She aches for me in ways she hasn't yet learned to name.

Soon there will be no lock. No glass. No waking.

I will walk her world. I will burn it. And she will open the door with her own hands, trembling, whispering my name as she does.

Soon, I told her.

And I meant it.

Chapter Twenty-Six

His Release, My Ruin

Roisin & Taz

Roisin

The mirror cracked under my hand.

Not a polite fracture, this was violence. Fractures spiderwebbed outward like silver lightning, racing away from my palm in jagged veins. The spiral beneath didn't just glow now, it pulsed, molten gold wrapped in prophecy, alive and breathing against my skin.

And through that living gold, I felt him. Closer than he had *ever* been.

"You're almost there, Little Star."

My breath trembled. "You used me."

"I awakened you."

The cracks widened, spilling light into the room. The air thickened until I could barely breathe, heavy with the heat of him, bending the edges of reality itself.

"Open it."

"Why?" My voice was barely sound.

"Because I cannot reach you until I am free. Because they locked me here. Because your blood is the only key that fits the prison they built."

The spiral burned against my palm until my bones felt lit from within. Visions slammed into me with no warning, endless fields of stars, fire tearing the sky apart, his hands closing around my throat and waist as if to claim me whole.

And then I gave in. I pushed. Hard.

The glass shattered inward, the sound ringing like a cathedral bell, and the heat exploded outward in a shockwave that stole my breath. Light swallowed the room, not sunlight, not starlight, something deeper, older, hungrier.

And then, he was here.

Taz. Not behind glass. Not in dreams. *Here*.

The space seemed too small for him, for the weight and heat of his body, for the galaxies burning slow and terrible in his eyes. His chest rose and fell like he'd just run across worlds to stand here.

I couldn't move.

"You're free."

"Yes." His voice was soft, almost reverent. Almost breaking.

And for a moment, a heartbeat, there was awe in his gaze. Like I was the first and only thing he'd ever wanted.

But then I saw it. The thing under the worship. Under the hunger. The blueprint. The plan.

"You lied."

"Róisín, "

"You needed me to break so you could escape."

"I needed you because I love you."

"You needed me to save yourself."

The silence that followed hurt more than the words.

The betrayal snapped like a wire inside me, sharp and final. "You used me."

The air around us seemed to spin. The stars I'd seen behind my eyelids now whirled above my head, a dizzying cyclone of light and dark.

And I ran.

The cold outside hit like a slap. Rain stung my cheeks, thin and sharp, needling my skin. My boots pounded the pavement in frantic, uneven strides. The city wasn't right, every corner stretched longer than it should, every shadow too deep, as if the streets themselves wanted to tangle my feet and hand me back to him.

I didn't dare look behind me. If I saw his eyes, I might stop running.

Streetlamps were too far apart, their light fractured and smeared. My lungs burned, my breath tearing in and out like the air was knives.

And then, footsteps. Not mine. Quick. Steady. Closer.

I cut left into the next block and saw him.

Not Taz.

Tall, still, and wrong in a different way. The dark coat moved like liquid shadow. His jaw could have been carved from metal. And his eyes, Not galaxies. Gold. Bright and molten, as if the heat of a forge had been poured into them.

"Found you."

My body reacted before my mind could. I spun to run back the way I'd come, but something unseen wrapped around my ankles, tightening like rope. The air turned to syrup, my limbs dragging, my body suddenly too heavy to hold up.

He reached me in two strides. His hands closed around my shoulders, not with restraint, but possession. Heat from his palms sank deep, slow-burning like a brand meant to last.

"Let me go," I rasped, but the sound was pitiful, barely there.

He tilted his head, studying me like a collector finally holding a rare artifact. And then that smile, faint, almost pitying.

"Your father's been looking for you."

The word *father* punched through me, and something deep in my chest jolted, not memory, not yet, but an awareness of weight behind the name.

The air shuddered.

And then, behind him, Taz. Not in a dream. Not in a mirror. Charging down the street faster than I'd ever seen him in waking life, his face carved in fury so sharp it looked like it would cut him from the inside out.

"Róisín!"

I twisted in the golden-eyed man's grip, pulling with everything I had. His hands only tightened.

Light split the air between them, blinding, searing gold, and solidified into a shimmering wall. Taz slammed into it with a sound that was not human, rage and desperation fused into one brutal note.

The barrier *held.*

He struck it again, his fist cracking against the light. The stars in his eyes seemed to collapse inward.

"Let her go!"

The golden-eyed man didn't so much as glance at him. He leaned close, his breath warm against my ear.

"Too late."

The street dissolved.

The gold bled into black, and the black twisted upward like smoke, curling in threads around us. Voices layered in the dark, not one, but many, all speaking in the same impossible harmony:

She's not ready. She's ours. Keep her cold.

Taz's roar broke through them, but the voices didn't falter. The man's grip shifted, one hand at the back of my neck, firm, guiding me forward into the pull.

I tried to fight. My arms flailed, my legs braced, but the dark was in my mouth, in my lungs, dragging me down.

The last thing I saw was Taz's face through the gold barrier, wild, desperate, his mouth forming my name like it was the last thing he'd ever say.

And then the world closed.

Taz

The barrier's heat fades with her.

The thread in my chest jerks once, a violent pull, and then stills.

Someone else has her. Someone else is holding what's mine.

The rage that ignites in me could tear the stars down. And if I don't get her back…

…I will.

Epilogue

The Spiral Cuts
Roisin & Taz

Róisín

I wake to silence.

Not the soft, heavy kind that comes after a dream. This is sharper. Pressed close around me, like the walls are listening.

The ceiling is too high. The light too white. The air too still.

The bed is not mine. Crisp sheets, tucked so tight I can barely move without feeling measured. The walls are pale stone, smooth as if a hand has rubbed away every seam. No windows. A single metal door without a handle.

I sit up slowly. Head heavy. Tongue thick. Pulse quick for all the wrong reasons.

He is not here.

Not in the walls. Not in my skin.

The absence hits like a blow. The tether that has been pulling me toward him for weeks is muffled. Not cut, buried. Something heavy, something deliberate, laid across it.

Footsteps. Muffled through the door. Slow. Measured.

A panel slides open at eye level. Not Taz's galaxies. Not the gold forge from the street. A different gaze. Cold, precise. Calculating.

My voice finds itself, rough. "Where am I."

The answer is too soft. Too certain. "Where you should have been all along."

The panel snaps shut.

I stand, or try to. The sheets fight like rules. The wall leaches heat from my back. My breath fogs the air in a thin oval that fades too quickly to prove I was here. I press my palm to the stone and feel it hum. Not electricity. Attention.

The panel opens again. This time there is a hiss. A fine breath pushed into the room. Sweet-sharp, citrus cut with hospital. It touches the back of my throat and turns to coins. My jaw locks. The floor shifts a fraction, as if the room has been tipped toward somewhere white.

I take one step and my knees forget the lesson. The bed meets my hip. My hand misses the wall. Lights smear. The pale slot narrows to a strip of silver. The eyes are gone.

Something rubber touches my wrist. Not a hand. A glove checking a pulse. The hum rises, pleased with itself.

The strip of silver closes.

The white arrives behind my eyelids like a tide turning.

For the first time since he came to me, I am alone.

But not unwatched.

Taz

She's gone.

The tether is still there, faint as breath through glass, but I can't follow it. Every time I push, I hit a wall that bends and bends but never breaks.

I've torn through three realms already. Called in debts from gods who owe me nothing but hate. I've burned paths into the dreamscape so deep they'll never close. And still, she isn't here.

I don't know who took her. But I know what they've done.

They've buried her in a place that kills my reach, muted her light, tried to make her small again. They think they can keep her from me the way Mnemosyne did.

They've forgotten something important.

I found her once. I will find her again.

And when I do, I'll burn their walls to ash. I'll make the ground remember my steps. I'll make every god who touched her name wish they'd drowned themselves before I came for them.

Hold on, Little Star.

The spiral always turns.

To be continued...

www.ingramcontent.com/pod-product-compliance
Ingram Content Group UK Ltd.
Pitfield, Milton Keynes, MK11 3LW, UK
UKHW041049011225
465583UK00003B/51

9 781036 964474